Malarkey

Also by Keith Gray

Warehouse
Happy

31/10/06

Malarkey

for Archie

All best

Keith Gray

Keith Gray

RED FOX DEFINITIONS

MALARKEY

A RED FOX BOOK 978 0 099 43944 8
0 099 43944 1

First published in Great Britain by Red Fox,
an imprint of Random House Children's Books

This edition published 2003

5 7 9 10 8 6

Typeset in 12/14.5 Bembo by Palimpsest Book Production Limited,
Polmont, Stirlingshire

Red Fox Books are published by Random House Children's Books,
61–63 Uxbridge Road, London W5 5SA,
a division of The Random House Group Ltd,
in Australia by Random House Australia (Pty) Ltd,
20 Alfred Street, Milsons Point, Sydney, NSW 2061, Australia,
in New Zealand by Random House New Zealand Ltd,
18 Poland Road, Glenfield, Auckland 10, New Zealand,
and in South Africa by Random House (Pty) Ltd,
Isle of Houghton, Corner of Boundary Road & Carse O'Gowrie,
Houghton 2198, South Africa

THE RANDOM HOUSE GROUP Limited Reg. No. 954009
www.kidsatrandomhouse.co.uk

A CIP catalogue record for this book is available from the British Library.

Printed and bound in Great Britain by
Cox & Wyman Ltd, Reading, Berkshire

Thanks to made-up people such as
John McClane, John Rebus and Philip Marlowe.
And to the 100% real people
Carolyn, Charlie, Harriet, Jasmine and Steve.

CONTENTS

THE WRONG PERSON
IN THE WRONG PLACE
AT THE WRONG TIME

ONE

A Thursday, about half-past ten, and already my brain was frozen. I blamed double maths with Mr Macallan. Wet break meant the cloakroom was packed and noisy with every conversation about who'd done what to whom, who was going to, and who wouldn't dare, being shouted. I wanted a little space to help my head thaw. I wanted a cigarette to get the defrosting started. There were too many dripping cagoules, too many squeaky trainers on the damp floor, and the fluorescent lights were losing their struggle to dig the corridor out of its gloomy dimness. Maybe it was just the mood I was in, but summer seemed such a long, long way off.

Brook High is a great grey concrete ants' nest of a school, with well over two thousand of us scurrying around between lessons, so 'a little space' is always going to be difficult to come by. I had my bag with me – it was a bulky black holdall, and I used it like a bulldozer's blade to push a way through the hubbub. I hadn't gone more than two steps when a hand reached out to grab me.

'Are you Malarkey?' A slim, dark-haired girl in a customized school uniform had hold of my arm and wouldn't let go. 'You're John Malarkey, right?'

I nodded. 'Yeah, I'm Malarkey.'

I tried to think if I might have seen her before. I'd not even been at Brook for two weeks yet, and there were so many kids, different ones in each of my classes, that I'd been finding it difficult to pin anyone down to talk to more than once. This girl looked about my age, about sixteen, so could easily have sat behind me in maths or English.

Her clothes weren't exactly school ruling, but were passable as Brook colours – enough to keep most of the teachers from complaining anyway. And I liked the way she wore them, making it look as though she'd bought an individual outfit rather than a dictated uniform. She wasn't quite as tall as me, but was by far prettier. She had a perfect beauty spot on her right cheek that could have been make-up. Still, I didn't recognize her. 'Who're you?'

She didn't answer, but at least let go of me. She turned to look over her shoulder and rose up on her tiptoes, searching for someone in the crowd. 'He's here,' she called, signalling, waving and pointing at me. 'This is him.'

I grabbed hold of *her* now. 'What's going on?' I didn't like the idea of being singled out.

She squirmed free of my grip and stepped away from me, slipping easily in among the crowd again. I went to follow her, but was suddenly, roughly, shoved from behind.

'Hey!'

I was clattered against the lockers. The crowd withdrew like greasy water, with me as the single drop of Fairy Liquid at its centre. A kick in the back of my knee buckled my leg and sent me down.

'*Hey!*'

I tried to turn round, but was thumped hard between the shoulders and pushed face first to sprawl on the wet, dirty floor. My bag was snatched away from me. All I saw were the speedy heels of identical trainers as my attackers took off along the corridor.

Maybe it wasn't a fist that had hit me, I was thinking; maybe it was a bus. I used the lockers for support and stifled a groan as I got to my feet. Everybody was staring at me, but no one moved to help. There were two lads running towards the stairs; one blond, one dark and spiky – the blond-haired kid carried my bag.

'They've got my bag!' I said. Still nobody moved; they just kept their distance. I looked, but couldn't see the girl with the perfect beauty spot among any of the blank faces. The two lads were up the stairs out of sight. 'They've got my bag,' I repeated, almost as an explanation this time, because I'd realized it was up to me alone to give chase.

Not that I was sure my legs were going to make it. They were shaky, untrustworthy with the shock of what had just happened. Thankfully life returned to them as I pounded down the corridor. I shoved the gawping statues out of my way and made certain I didn't lose sight of those identical trainers. I leaped up the stairs two at a time, mindful of the wet footprints, wary of slipping. I could feel the shape of my mobile phone in my coat pocket so I knew there wasn't anything particularly valuable in my bag – apart from my Walkman, I suppose – but that wasn't the point. I swung around the banister at the first-floor landing and charged past the classrooms.

The floor was swarming with Year Eight kids. 'Get out of the way!' They flattened themselves up against the lockers. '*Move!*' Anybody who didn't got a shoulder or an elbow as I charged through. '*Get out of the way!*' I knocked one lad flat.

Blondie seemed to have the same idea and crashed through the middle of a group of five or six with my bag swinging like a weapon. Two of the group were taken by surprise, barged to the floor with arms and legs flailing, skidding across the damp tiles. They saw me coming and tried to scramble away. I managed to hurdle over them, windmilling my arms as I leaped, and somehow keep my own feet underneath me. People were staring; I sped by them all, keeping my eyes on Blondie and my bag.

The corridor turned sharp left, with a notice board on the facing wall full of timetables, Reading Club information and posters of celebrities grinning over the tops of their favourite books. I was running too fast: I skidded and had to hit the board to try and bounce myself round the corner. Several drawing pins jumped free, posters fell and fluttered down. The spiky-haired kid was waiting for me just round the bend. Maybe if I'd had time to think I would have stood my ground for a fight, but sheer momentum forced me to put my head down and keep going.

He looked like he was expecting a fight. I barrelled into him. He was twice as wide as me and took my shoulder in his chest with a grunt. I hoped I hurt his chest as much as he hurt my shoulder, and he tumbled backwards, arms flailing. Sweet revenge, I thought as he thudded onto his backside.

Blondie was still up ahead of me with my bag over his shoulder; he jinked left, then dived through an already open door and into the library. I was gaining on him. I was going to get the bastard! My heart pounded as loud as my feet. A few seconds later I was through that door too.

The librarian was incredulous, bawling at us as we darted between the shelves. She sprang out from behind her desk to grab hold of us, but we were too quick. 'What on *earth* do you think you are doing?' Blondie ran through the middle of the homework tables, flinging chairs behind him to block me. I stumbled over them, only just managed to stay upright. 'Stop right there!' the librarian shouted. Little kids cowered behind large reference books. I chased Blondie from one end to the other, quite literally from A to Z, and through the red fire door. 'Out of bounds!' the librarian yelled. 'Those stairs are out of bounds!'

I was breathing hard, my chest hurt, but I was still gaining. I didn't have my heavy bag to struggle with. Blondie was leaping down the teachers' stairs; I was hot on his heels, although it wasn't just my bag I was chasing. I also wanted to know why. I'd been picked out, *selected*, and I wanted to know *why*.

I banged through the fire exit and heard the librarian screaming again. I realized it must be Spike, back on his feet and not all that far behind. Certainly not far enough for my liking.

These stairs led up to the roof so students weren't supposed to use them. I chased Blondie down, however. I had one hand on the metal banister, the other up against the rough plaster wall for balance. I was leaping down two and three steps at a time, my feet loud and echoing. Spike was above me. I didn't have a clue where these stairs came out at the bottom; I wished I knew the school better. I saw the top of Blondie's head as he reached the ground floor and was through a door without stopping. I was two thumps of my pounding heart behind him, hoping I wasn't being led into some blind alley where he and Spike would have me trapped.

But we were outside on the flat and empty tennis courts – it would be another month before the nets went up. The rain pelted down from a sky that could also have been tarmac. We charged through the puddles; I was soaked in seconds.

My heavy bag wasn't slowing Blondie down as much as I'd hoped. He was heading for the gym block, and I was trying to figure out why. Was there somewhere he could hide? I heard the door from the teachers' stairs slam back on its hinges and realized Spike was closer than ever. I could almost feel his hot breath on the back of my neck.

Blondie was across the muddy patch of grass and onto the path, then through the double doors into the gym block. He dropped my bag and immediately spun round to lock the doors after him. There were bolts top and bottom and he shoved them home with a bang, leaving me to rattle at the handles uselessly. He pushed his smug face up against the glass panels and leered at me, the criss-cross of the safety wire inside making him look like an ugly jigsaw puzzle. He picked my bag up and taunted me by swinging it at his side.

'What do you want it for?' I shouted through the glass, through heaving breaths. 'It's full of books, and I'm betting a fiver you can't even read.'

He showed me the Vs. Then his eyes flicked over my shoulder, and at the same instant I saw Spike's reflection in the glass as he loomed up behind me. I turned as quickly as I could and tried to raise my fists. He hit me like a truck.

I was thrown clean off my feet – I flew. But not very far.

Every bone in my body rattled as I crashed down onto the pavement, the wind going out of me in a painful *whoomph* of breath, leaving a second or two of fuzzy greyness at the edges of my vision. Spike raised his foot as if to stamp on me. He was wearing black Adidas. I immediately recognized the famous stripes even though he'd tried to paint over one of them. The trainers should have had three white stripes displayed on the side, but for some reason he'd blacked out one of these stripes so that now only two could be seen clearly.

I rolled into a ball, pulling my arms over my head, waiting for his foot to fall.

'Stay down,' he growled. He was panting like a bull. 'Stay down and you'll get your bag back.'

I was surprised he didn't follow through and finish me off; he sure as hell looked like he wanted to. 'What do you want it for? There's nothing in it except school stuff.' I went to uncurl, wanting to be back up and eye to eye with him as soon as possible.

He immediately raised his trainer again. 'Stay *down!*' He held his foot close to my face.

So I didn't move, but stared hard at him, refused to take my eyes off him. It was all the defiance I had. I might have knocked him down once, but this was the second time I'd been on the floor at his feet. The rain splashed all around me and I stayed where I was until he'd slowly lowered his foot.

He gestured to his friend. 'Let me in.'

Blondie didn't seem too sure.

But Spike looked at me curled up on the ground – sweating, out of breath, soaked to the skin – and he laughed. 'He's not going to do anything.'

Blondie laughed right along with him, and swung the door wide. I felt their laughter claw along the length of my spine, making me shudder, making me grit my teeth in frustration.

They re-bolted the door again so I couldn't try to follow. I tentatively picked myself up. It was almost as if they'd forgotten me now. They sauntered away along the corridor in between the changing rooms with their backs to me. If I'd managed to be an inconvenience, then I'd been lucky.

I was wet and cold. I didn't want to back down, but neither did I want to stand out here getting wetter and colder in the hope they'd come out again at the end of break. I couldn't understand why my bag was so important – why pick me from the crowd? Was it simply because I was the new kid?

'You boy!' Some teacher or other was standing at the door to the teachers' stairs; I guessed the librarian had probably sent him after us. 'You boy, come here!' He hovered in the doorway, wanting me to go to him because he wasn't willing to come out into the rain. I didn't want to waste my time telling a teacher what had happened. You didn't get to Year Eleven without realizing that no matter what the crime against you, grassing was a sure-fire way of aggravating the problem. So I ignored him, heading back across the tennis courts but ducking inside through the students' entrance instead. I was too new for him to know my face, and the school was too big for him to recognize me again.

I went straight to the toilets, where I could keep out of the way until the end of break and maybe sneak a quick cigarette. I waited for a lad who didn't bother to wash his hands, then the place was empty.

I fished inside my jacket for my fags and lighter, only to swear loudly when I found a pocket full of tobacco flakes. I must have squashed the pack underneath me; the cigarettes were all crushed and broken. I told myself I was meant to be giving up anyway, but . . . But reckoned one would have been so welcome right now, because it would have been the kind with hardly any guilt-trip attached. And they were the ones that tasted best. After being knocked about and having my bag stolen I *deserved* a cigarette, yet all I had was a pocket full of twisted paper and flakes. Could things get any worse?

In the stained mirror above the sinks I looked pale and defeated: my face was red and blotchy, my hair plastered to my forehead. My eyes were still angry, however, and I liked that I could still see some fire there, no matter how ineffective.

I admit I was tempted to go home, to just walk out, but it's true that I hated backing down. I don't think it's arrogance; it's just that I've never been particularly good at it.

All I could do was wash the mud off my cheek and try to dry my hair with the paper hand towels. Maybe I really would get my bag back, with or without its contents. Stranger things had happened. I had another pack of Marlboro Lights in my locker, and that was where I was going. But when the bell rang I realized I didn't have time. Reluctantly I headed straight for my next lesson instead.

History was on the second floor. I got the feeling I was collecting whispers and sideways glances as I made my way up the stairs, but couldn't tell if it was because everybody knew what had happened, or simply because I looked like I lived in bus shelters. Whichever, I managed to ignore most of it. I was thinking about the girl, the one with the perfect beauty spot. I wanted to know what she had to do with all of this, if anything. Why she'd pointed me out, and how come she knew my name.

I still wasn't sure whether she was in one of my classes or not, so I looked for her as soon as I walked into the history room. She wasn't there. But my bag was.

The shock of it actually pinned me to the spot, and I only got moving again thanks to a nudge from behind because I was blocking the door. My black holdall was sitting on my desk in the back row of the classroom. Shock and then paranoia, because somebody in the room might have put it there. Somebody definitely must have seen who did.

A quick glance around the room, but nobody seemed to be paying me much attention – too busy chatting loudly and ferreting around in their own bags for books and pens and pencils. I approached my holdall like it was a bomb, sliding slowly onto the seat behind my desk. Miss Walker came in, started taking the register, and had to call my name twice before I realized and answered. Again I checked to see if I was being watched, but all heads were turned forward. I unzipped the bag's main compartment, without actually pulling it towards me. It didn't go bang, obviously, and I started checking to see what had been stolen.

Mr Macallan burst into the room without knocking. 'I'm sorry to interrupt your lesson, Miss Walker. I want to have a word with the students who were in my maths lesson before break.'

I looked up at him briefly from rooting through my books and files. He was a tall, fidgety man with a thick black beard. He had one of those heads that could be turned upside down and still look exactly the same, like in those comedy pictures. Behind his beard today, however, his cheeks were flushed, and his tie was thrown over one shoulder as if he'd been running against the wind. He towered over Miss Walker's dumpy, pear-shaped figure, and quite honestly didn't seem to give a damn about interrupting her lesson. He didn't wait for her to answer before he bellowed at us.

'I want to see anybody who was in my lesson in room thirteen periods one and two.' He had a register of his own. 'That's Briggs, Brown, Fassl, Games, Hudson, Klein, Lindsey and Malarkey.'

Nobody moved at first, unsure of what was happening.

I was still in my bag, amazed that nothing seemed to be missing – even my Walkman and CDs were still there. But underneath my maths books I spotted something I didn't recognize, something that wasn't mine and hadn't been there before: small, flat, brown, made of leather.

'Come on, come on!' Mr Macallan was agitated. 'Bring your coats and bags.' His cheeks flushed a deeper, angrier red behind his beard, and I knew what he was going to say next before he even opened his mouth. 'My wallet has been stolen, and I believe it's someone from this morning's lesson who's taken it.'

I knew because it was the small, flat, brown, leather thing at the bottom of my bag.

TWO

What else could I do? I held the wallet up for Mr Macallan to see. 'I've got it,' I said.

All faces turned to me. And the silence in the room was the sound of spectators at a firing squad.

Mr Macallan's eyes widened to take aim, then narrowed to shoot me right where I was sitting. The flushed red of his cheeks deepened, looking so hot and angry that I expected his black beard to smoulder and smoke to curl from his nostrils. He said, 'Bring it here,' pointing to a spot by his feet. 'And I can assure you, laddie,' he continued, 'that you're in twice the amount of trouble you think you're in if there's anything missing.'

I hadn't thought about that, and realized I maybe should have checked to make sure there was still cash and credit cards inside. Not that I would have been able to know for sure, but if it was empty I probably wouldn't have been quite so eager to wave it above my head. I squeezed it gently as I climbed out of my seat, and it felt fat enough, but who could tell?

'*Now*, laddie!'

I did as I was told, with everyone's stares following my every move. I held the wallet out and the maths teacher snatched it from me. I watched his fingers as he riffled through the contents, pausing once, twice. Even from where I was standing I could see the tatty edges of five- and ten-pound notes – which only added to the mystery of the whole thing in my eyes. What was the point in stealing a wallet if you didn't take the cash? His fingers stopped to pluck a small, glossy square of paper from one of the leather pockets. He frowned at it for what seemed like a long, long time.

'Maybe I should take Mr Malarkey outside,' he said to Miss Walker, who was clearly very disappointed with me indeed. He stepped through the doorway out into the corridor and waited for me to follow him. I did, and the rest of the class burst into chatter, but Miss Walker hushed them quickly as she hurried the door shut after us.

Mr Macallan waited for the click of the closed door then handed me the square of paper. 'Does your juvenile mind find this amusing?'

It was a photograph, only small, but you could clearly see what I assumed to be the maths teacher's wife and two young daughters sitting under a tree on a sunny day, grinning happily for the camera. And the problem was, yes, my juvenile mind did find it amusing, because someone had given the three of them big black beards to match Mr Macallan's. It was an uncanny resemblance.

I shrugged. 'I didn't do it,' I said.

He ignored me, opening the folds of his wallet to show me the gap in the paraphernalia he expected me to recognize. 'I don't know what benefit you think my video club membership card and driving licence will be to you, but I want them returned immediately, do you understand?'

I was as surprised as he was. Who needed a video club membership card more than they needed cash?

'*Do you understand?*'

'I haven't got them,' I told him, wondering how much he was going to believe.

He thrust the wallet under my nose, frothing over with barely controlled anger. 'Then where are they, laddie? Where are they, eh?'

I shrugged. Here went nothing. I said, 'Two lads stole my bag at break. There's a whole bunch of witnesses. They knocked me around a bit, took my bag, but when I went to history they'd returned it; left it on my desk. I found your wallet inside.'

He eyed me deliberately. 'Who were these boys?'

'I don't know. Year Ten or Eleven, probably.'

'Why did they steal your bag only to return it again?'

'I don't know.'

'And why would these conscientious thieves give you my wallet?'

There wasn't anything else I could say. 'I don't know.'

He shook his head at me. 'I think we should see what Mr Coleburn has to say about it, don't you?' He ordered me with a sharp gesture to walk with him down the corridor.

Again I did as I was told. He stayed a pace behind and I had to glance over my shoulder to ask, 'Who's Mr Coleburn?'

'He's your Head of Year, laddie. And the first step on the surprisingly short road to exclusion starts with him.'

Oh, I thought. Marvellous.

I was marched to the ground floor, past the main entrance and into the part of the school known as Top Block. It was newer than the main block; the corridors were wider and better lit, with graffiti-free walls painted a soothing blue. This was the part of the school parents and visitors always got to see. The music room, drama hall and lecture theatre were in this block, but Mr Macallan marched me past all three. Underneath yet another set of stairs was a closed door with 'MR COLEBURN' lettered in white at about eye level. The maths teacher rapped on it sharply. After two seconds' silence he knocked again.

He glared at me as if it was my fault the Head of Year wasn't home. 'You.' He pointed at me. 'Stay here.' He pointed at an exact spot on the corridor floor. 'Don't move from that spot.' But he didn't trust me; he obviously thought I'd do a runner the second his back was turned. 'I'm warning you, laddie,' he warned me, wagging a finger as he ushered me inside.

I could tell he wasn't happy about what he was doing. Leaving me, a suspected thief (probably already convicted in his mind), in Mr Coleburn's office was kind of risky. Who knew what my sticky fingers might find? But what else could he do with me?

'Straighten up your uniform,' he ordered me, as though being allowed into the Head of Year's office was a special occasion that you should get dressed up for. 'The state of you isn't going to impress Mr Coleburn.'

You wouldn't look so good if you'd been forced to roll in the dirt either, I thought. But instead I said, 'I didn't take your wallet, Mr Macallan.'

He searched my face in that deliberate way again. 'Why was it in your bag?' he asked.

'I don't know.'

He harrumphed at me. 'If I were you, I wouldn't set a single foot outside of this office even if it caught fire. Do you understand? And don't touch anything – nothing, do you hear? Nothing.'

He hovered for a moment longer, still not liking what

he was doing. Then at last left, closing the door behind him.

I was tempted to walk out. I hovered just like the maths teacher had. But realized it could easily be seen as an admission of guilt. I swore under my breath, and got ready to stand my ground, hoping the Head of Year would see things my way.

The office was a small, carpeted room, particularly neat and tidy. The window gave a view of the teachers' car park. It looked as though the rain was finally letting up, the sky was clearing a little, but the Venetian blinds were half down and I was tempted to switch the light on. I decided against it, however, unsure of Mr Coleburn's reaction if it appeared I'd been nosing around, so stood there feeling like an intruder.

I'd be lying if I said I wasn't nervous. Not overly so, because I was reckoning on all those witnesses who'd seen what had happened at break to back me up – even the shouty librarian should remember me. But I was wary. Because I didn't know what was going on. Ever felt like part of a bigger picture you can't quite see?

Mr Coleburn's large pale-wood desk had a comfy chair behind for him, and a hard plastic one for his interrogatee. The expanse of desktop was ordered with maybe a dozen piles of papers, most of which were underneath exotic paperweights – arty, colourful domes and pyramids; the pens and pencils all lived in their natty, tubular holder. Box files on the shelf on the back wall were clearly and appropriately labelled; on top of the grey filing cabinet was some green plant or other with fat, rubbery leaves. On the back of the door hung a large calendar, each month a different landscape photograph – hill, lake, forest. I guessed it was the kind of thing that was needed if you spent your life trapped within Brook's grey walls.

A tapping at the window surprised me, and I peered under the blind to see a lad with fair hair cropped so close he looked smooth and bald. 'Let us in,' he mouthed, grinning, miming for me to open the window.

I just looked at him.

He was eager to get in. 'Come on.' He winked and grinned.

I hooked a thumb over my shoulder at the door. 'It's open.' But he didn't seem to understand. And it really had nothing to do with me anyway, so I turned back to the calendar.

He banged hard on the window, and when I looked at him a second time, he lifted up his foot to point at his trainer. He wanted me to see exactly what type he was wearing – it seemed important to him. It was a pair of black Adidas. So Blondie, Spike, and now this guy all had the same taste in training shoes – although he hadn't coloured in any of his stripes. Even so, he was certainly insistent I took a close look. And because I'm not a great believer in coincidence, I flipped the catch and lifted the bottom half of the window up as high as the blind, but blocked him from climbing in.

'Who're you?'

He frowned at me. 'What?'

'Who are you? What's your name?'

'Dominic,' he said. Then quickly changed his mind. 'Dom.'

'Okay, Dominic Dom, tell me why I should let you in.'

His frown deepened: this obviously wasn't what he'd

expected. 'You what? Just let us in, will you?' He tried to push against me.

'Either give me a good reason for letting you into the Head of Year's office,' I told him. 'Or get lost.'

Dominic Dom grinned smugly. 'I know who stole your bag,' he said.

'Well, that's good enough for me,' I admitted, and stepped to one side.

He scrambled over the windowsill. I wondered how long he'd been out there, because his clothes were damp and when he ran a hand over his shorn hair the rain that had been trapped in the stubble ran down the back of his neck. He shivered with it. 'Is Coleburn still in the main block?' he asked. He was taller than me, but even though he was nurturing a bum-fluff moustache, I guessed he was younger. He was nervy, skittish, and not doing a particularly good job of hiding it.

'I'm not sure where he is,' I said. 'Mr Macallan's gone to find him.'

Dominic Dom pulled a face. 'I hate Macallan. He does my head in.' He was over by the desk. 'How long's he been gone?'

'Not long,' I said. Then: 'So who stole my bag?'

He ignored me. He was peering at the stacks of paper on the desk. Careful not to make a mess or disturb anything too much, he started lifting the domes and pyramids to flip through the pages underneath. 'Put the light on for us a minute, will you?'

'Who stole my bag?' I repeated.

'It's not stolen if you got it back, is it?' he said.

Which I guessed was true enough. I said, 'I like your trainers.'

He looked up at me suddenly, then his eyes flicked down to my own trainers. Converse. He seemed hesitant now. '*I* like them,' he said slowly.

I shrugged. 'Bit common for my tastes.'

He wanted to answer me back, but thought better of it and returned to searching the desktop. I watched him, wondering what he was looking for. He was being extremely fussy about replacing everything after he'd touched it. I wanted to find out if he really did know something about what was going on.

'It's in the second drawer from the bottom,' I told him.

He frowned. 'What is?'

'The thing you're looking for.' I pointed at the desk. 'Second drawer. In there.'

He was tempted to believe me; he almost looked up at me again. 'Just shut up, will you?' I was making him more nervous. He turned his back on me and started going through the filing cabinet.

I was deliberately trying to wind him up, to see if he'd let anything slip. 'Where did you get your trainers from?' I asked.

He ignored me. One of the filing cabinet drawers jammed and he swore under his breath, struggling to push it home again.

'Why does everybody wear the same trainers around here?' I stayed standing exactly where I was, not wanting to get within reaching distance – or within hitting distance. 'Was Mr Macallan's wallet a gift? Does his wife really need to shave?'

The swearing became a steady stream. With a sudden jerk and a squeak of metal the filing cabinet drawer slid home. He trapped his finger and yelped. The green plant on top wobbled precariously but didn't fall.

I said, 'My name's David, by the way.'

Now he was looking at me. 'What?' He sucked on his finger. The expression on his face was all worried confusion, like a dog that's been told you've given its favourite bone to next door's cat.

I held out a hand for him to shake. 'David Smith. Pleased to meet you.'

He was wise to me quick enough, and his lip curled in a sneer. 'I know who you are.'

'Who's that then?' I asked.

'You're the new kid: Malarkey.'

I held up my hands in submission. '*Everybody* seems to know my name,' I admitted. And although I wasn't about to let it show, it made me very uneasy.

The lad gave a noise of triumph as he found whatever it was he'd been searching for in the bottom drawer of the filing cabinet. He stuffed the thin, blue pocket file up his jumper and tucked it into the waistband of his trousers to stop it from falling out.

'What's that, then?' I asked.

But he wasn't about to tell me. He was back at the window, one leg already outside in the fresh air.

'What's wrong with doors all of a sudden?' I asked.

He gave me a look like *I* was the one acting strange. 'Do you think I want to walk right into Coleburn or something?'

I shrugged. 'So who stole my bag?' I tried one last time.

He was all cocky and brave now he'd got what he came for. 'My mates.' He swung his other leg out of the window.

I made a grab for his arm, not wanting to let him disappear without telling me what was going on. He was quick and slippery: he wriggled out of my grip and shoved me hard in the chest, making me stagger backwards into Mr Coleburn's desk. I lost my footing and almost sprawled backwards across it, knocking one of the paperweights to the floor with a *thunk*, scattering the papers that had been held underneath.

Dominic Dom thought this was one of the funniest things he'd ever seen. 'See-ya, wouldn't want to be-ya,' he said with a lairy grin, then slammed the window down and was gone.

I was getting pretty bloody fed up with being pushed around. And was one hundred per cent pretty bloody hacked off with myself for letting it happen.

I tried to see where Dominic Dom was running, but he was quick and kept his head down, and disappeared round the side of the building. I was tempted to leap out of the window after him; only just managed to hold myself back. That wouldn't be the smartest move. I knew I had a decision to make. The teachers would be here any minute – did I tell them what had just happened?

I started to gather up the papers and letters I'd scattered, but wondered whether to simply leave them as they were and tell Mr Coleburn that it was all Dominic Dom's doing. I peered at the desktop myself, checked under a couple of the paperweights just like he had, had a quick look in the filing cabinet too, but there was no telling what he'd taken. What could have been in the blue pocket file he'd stolen? I didn't have the foggiest.

I found myself neatening up the stack of paper. I wasn't going to say anything.

A few reasons why not sprang to mind. One big one being that I'd let him in. I was in trouble anyway, and the fact that I'd opened the window for him, and stood there watching while he'd blatantly searched for and then stolen whatever it was, certainly wouldn't be a point in my favour. Secondly, I wanted to know what the hell was going on, and I doubted very much that teachers were going to be any kind of help. Teachers are always the last to find out what's happening at cloakroom level; most of them are deaf and blind once they set foot outside the classroom.

I made the decision, not at all sure if it was the right one. Spur of the moment. There was a chance it would backfire on me, end up making things worse – I knew that.

I straightened everything up as best I could – just hoping Mr Coleburn wouldn't notice. I remembered the paperweight I'd knocked onto the floor. It had rolled underneath the desk and I had to get down on my hands and knees, crawling on all fours to reach for it, its domed shape difficult to grip. I'd only just managed to get hold of it when I heard Mr Macallan's voice in the corridor outside.

I jumped, startled, guilty, nearly cracking my head on the underside of the desk. Shit! I scrambled backwards and leaped to my feet.

The two teachers strode in behind me. I stood very still. I hoped the paperweight-sized bulge in my pocket wasn't too obvious.

I recognized the Head of Year as soon as he flicked the light on. I'd seen him in and around Brook looking like a man who believed he was in control – looking like he believed he was Head of the Whole School, not just Year Eleven. He settled himself into his comfy chair on the opposite side of the desk before deigning to look at me.

'Sit down, laddie,' Mr Macallan ordered, pointing at the hard plastic chair. He was still holding his wallet in his hand, unwilling to let go of the evidence just yet.

I did as I was told reluctantly, because sitting down made me feel vulnerable. The wide expanse of the desktop seemed to shrink me in stature because the chair was very small, more like one from a primary school; my knees came up close to my chin, and I was forced to sit up as straight as possible so I could see over all those stacks of paper. Then, with one teacher eyeing me over the top of his steepled fingers while the other hovered at my back breathing heavily through his nose, I had never felt more like a scolded child.

'So,' Mr Coleburn said. 'So.' I saw the way he viewed the state of my uniform with a frown – he was as immaculately dressed as his office was tidy. Not fashionable, because there is a difference. But his grey hair was perfectly parted to one side, the size of the knot on his grey tie was just so, and his charcoal suit was a dry-cleaned dream. I realized the colourful paperweights probably had more personality. I was waiting for him to notice that his desk had been messed with, but he seemed far too interested in me for the time being. 'Well, this certainly isn't what you'd call the most auspicious beginning to your time with us, is it, John?' He raised his eyebrows at me.

I'm always amazed by how many teachers are willing to become their students' enemy. Surely it just makes everything an uphill struggle? But I took his condescension on the chin and said, 'I'm not sure what you want me to say.'

'Well, John. Mr Macallan has explained—'

'I told Mr Macallan—'

He held up a warning finger. 'I'd rather you didn't interrupt me, John.' He waited one second, then another, to make absolutely certain I was quiet. Only then did he continue. 'Mr Macallan has explained to me exactly what happened, both sides of the story, and I have to admit that I'm inclined to believe *his*.'

He paused as if waiting for me to jump in again, but I stayed quiet. He never once raised his voice above conversation level, as though shouting might make him appear out of control. And he wanted me to know he was in full control of this situation; his whole tone was aimed at making me feel small and naughty like a child.

'You're a bright young man, John,' he said, clearly not believing it himself. 'I'm sure you don't need me to tell you the seriousness of this matter. A matter which could quite easily go beyond these school walls, and ultimately involve the police.' He watched me to make sure his words were having the desired effect. 'Mr Macallan, however, has judiciously agreed that we can deal with the matter ourselves. *If* you return what you have stolen, that is.'

I waited one second, then another, to make sure it was okay for me to speak now. I said, 'At break, in the Year Eleven cloakroom, two lads jumped me and stole my bag. When I went to Miss Walker's lesson in room—'

Mr Coleburn looked bored, waved my words away with his hand. 'This isn't getting you very far, John,' he said quietly.

'I haven't got Mr Macallan's video club card or driver's licence or whatever. I—'

'You were caught red-handed,' the maths teacher growled from over my shoulder.

'Why didn't I steal the money too?' I asked.

'Maybe stealing Mr Macallan's wallet was just a dare,' Mr Coleburn said, looking as though he'd seen similar petty, childish games all too often before.

I was boring him and he prodded listlessly at one or two of the papers on his desk. I noticed him frown slightly at the stack I'd scattered and tried to tidy up. I could almost read the thoughts stirring in his mind, and fidgeted awkwardly on the hard plastic seat. I was staring at that stack of papers too. He moved one of his paperweights from another pile to put on top. Then moved it back again. He knew something was wrong, just wasn't sure what exactly.

'Why did I admit I had the wallet in the first place?' I said quickly, trying to draw his attention to me. Wanting him to look at me instead of his desk. The paperweight in my pocket bulged.

'Maybe to prove yourself, to be one of the gang,' he said, still staring at his desktop, trying to figure out what was different. 'Just a prank to fit in as the new boy.'

'Aw, come on!' I virtually shouted.

He jumped as if coming to attention, and his cloudy face darkened with real anger at my sudden outburst. I had his full attention now.

I didn't lower my voice. 'What about everybody who saw my bag being stolen from me?'

He scowled at me, but clearly wasn't interested in my excuses and straightened his already straight tie to prove it. 'It wouldn't surprise me if you managed to find however many friends who are willing to lie for you.'

It felt like I was walking a tightrope here. I breathed a silent sigh of relief to have the focus back on me instead of the desk, but I still wanted to prove my innocence with the wallet. 'Have you spoken to the librarian?' I turned to look at Mr Macallan. 'Can't you at least ask her about what happened?'

'I made a point of seeing Mrs Wright before I went to find Mr Coleburn,' the maths teacher said. 'And she remembers a bunch of hoodlums haring through her library, causing havoc. But she says you weren't the one doing the chasing. She says there was a boy who was chasing *you* and *your* friend.'

I hung my head. I could see now that I wasn't going to win this argument.

'And she wants a detention from you,' Mr Macallan added. 'Four o'clock, Monday afternoon.'

Better and better, I thought. Things just keep on getting better.

'This is not the right foot to start on at Brook High,' Mr Coleburn told me. He shook his head as though he was finding it difficult coming to terms with such a sad fact. 'Not the right foot at all. You have come to us at an awkward time of year, what with the Easter holidays starting at the end of next week, and then your GCSEs in June.' He sighed and rocked back in his chair. 'Everybody else in Year Eleven will be taking home their final report next Friday – for some, their final school report ever – and I was concerned that you, John, should also receive a report even though I know very little about you. I was going to rely on your subject teachers' statements, and give you as full a report as possible – because of how important I felt it would be for you.' He paused, to make certain I was listening. 'It's particularly unfortunate, don't you think, that this is my first impression of you, and the impression I'm going to have when I complete your report? You are a bad apple.'

The man made my skin crawl. I caught myself hoping Dominic Dom had stolen something *really* important. I wanted to get out of his office and smash his gaudy paperweight into a million pieces.

'Your parents are going to be extremely disappointed,' he told me.

'Parent,' I corrected him.

He glared at me. 'What was that?'

'Parent, singular. My *parent* is going to be extremely disappointed.'

His eyes flicked over my shoulder to Mr Macallan and the colour rose to his cheeks. 'Yes, well.' He recovered quickly, but didn't apologize. 'See me at lunch time,' he said. 'Be sure to bring Mr Macallan's property with you. I'm afraid that failure to do so will result in a phone call to the police.' He dismissed me with a waft of his wrist. 'I cannot abide thieves.'

I didn't move. The maths teacher opened the door behind me, but I stayed exactly where I was. I waited for the Head of Year to look up at me again. I met his eyes. 'I didn't steal Mr Macallan's wallet,' I said. But I'd said it so many times it was beginning to sound weak even to me.

I stood up (which was an effort from such a low seat) and walked back out into the corridor.

Mr Macallan followed me. He was still angry behind his beard, and he still sounded like a teacher – which was a relief after Mr Coleburn's pseudo social-worker condescension. 'Yours is a difficult story to believe, laddie,' he said.

'Depends how hard you try.'

'And your smart mouth won't help any,' he growled.

'How many times do I have to say I didn't do it?' I asked him.

'Lunch time,' he reminded me, and clutching his wallet tightly he stepped back into the Head of Year's office, closing the door in my face.

THREE

I stared hard at the closed door. How much trouble was I in? I didn't know. I believed Mr Coleburn's threats, yet wasn't sure what he could do with them. I was tempted to knock on the door, try to argue harder. But one of my pet hates has always been people who whine, '*It's not fair.*' I've never really trusted 'fair'. Right and wrong, yes. But 'fair' has always seemed kind of flimsy to me.

I turned to walk away, then once more wondered whether or not to tell Mr Coleburn about someone else being in his office this morning – someone he wouldn't abide. My best guess, however, was that the contents of that blue file weren't going to be particularly exciting. Probably just some dodgy homework, I reckoned; something Dominic Dom wanted back before any of the teachers laid eyes on it. Maybe there were offensive doodles in the margin of his English essay, scribbled pictures of Mr Coleburn committing unsavoury acts, and libellous graffiti. Who knew? But it was nothing to do with me – not really.

Of course, if the Head of Year realized the file had gone walkies he could blame me. It would be his easiest solution. But I was hoping it wouldn't be missed for a few days or so, maybe not until after Easter with any luck, and by then he wouldn't be able to remember that I was in his office at the time it had vanished. The only problem I had was the damning evidence of the paperweight in my pocket. I knew I'd have to dump it as soon as I got the chance, and preferably in a place far away from me.

Something that concerned me more, however: I wondered if Mr Coleburn was going to try to contact my mum. I knew he'd have a hard time of it if he did, because we still hadn't had the flat's telephone connected. We used our mobiles if we needed a quick word with each other; neither of us seemed too willing to let the outside world get in at us just yet. It was true that most days since we'd moved Mum had said, 'Right, first job today is to get that phone sorted.' But she hadn't quite got round to it so far. She'd busy herself unpacking for the shop and end up reading half the stock as the hours sneaked by. The second-hand bookshop had been her dream for as long as I could remember; she was happy making it come true. And I was happy watching her.

First I went to my locker to collect the pack of Marlboro Lights that was in there. I mean, who could give up on a day like today?

I also checked my watch – then immediately wished I hadn't. I didn't want to go back to Miss Walker's history class, but I needed my bag and there was only five minutes of the lesson left. My fingers played with the pack's cellophane seal. If I opened it, I'd be forced to take a cigarette out. If I took a cigarette out, I'd stay in the toilets and smoke it. Simple inevitability. The thing was I also knew it was going to be important to keep my nose as clean as possible from here on in because I didn't want to give any teacher any reason to distrust me.

So with a heavy sigh I told myself a quick smoke was going to have to wait. Then I made my way to Miss

Walker's room, hoping that when I eventually did have that much-deserved cigarette, it could only taste sweeter.

All eyes were on me the second I stepped through the classroom door and the teacher had a hard time bringing everyone's attention back to her. I knew there were only a few minutes before the bell – but those few minutes dragged.

Usually, I don't mind history. I like the way you can follow the threads of events back through time, and how everything connects up in the long run. I think of it as being kind of similar to a spider's web – tug on one thread, and it has an effect on all the others too. Today, however, I had my own spider's web of events on my mind. How was Mr Macallan's wallet connected to what Dominic Dom had taken from Mr Coleburn's office? I didn't like the answer when it came. I realized the main thread had to be me.

As soon as the bell rang most of the class were up on their feet, me included. Miss Walker had to raise her voice above the sudden chatter and noise of scraping chairs. 'There are still some of you who owe me coursework. This is your last chance, people; if you want me to mark it in time to be submitted before your exams then I have to have it by Monday's lesson, okay?' There were half-hearted nods and mumbles from some of the kids. 'And don't forget we haven't got a lesson tomorrow afternoon because of the football match, but I'll be here if anybody wants to hand work in. Or you can put it in my collection box in the library. But it has to be before the end of the day.'

She managed to catch my eye as I was filing out into

the corridor. I wanted to duck out past her, but as I'd said, I didn't mind history, and I'd never had any problems with Miss Walker. 'Do you know if you're fully up to date from your last school, John?'

'I think so, miss.' I knew for certain that I was, because the teachers at my last school had made sure of it.

When I'd told them I was moving they'd all pulled exactly the same disapproving face and said, 'It's an awkward time to start a new school, John.' I'd got on well at the school and the teachers had seemed reluctant to let anybody else at another school mess up the hard work they'd put into me over the past few years. They'd doubled up on my homework, even given me a couple of lunch-time lessons, just to make sure. And none of them had approved of the move; one or two even went as far as saying so. I knew Mum had a bit of a reputation for being 'flaky'. They must have rolled their eyes *en masse* in the staff room when they heard Jess Malarkey was dragging her son halfway across the country just before his GCSEs so she could set up a second-hand bookshop.

In fact, even now, Miss Walker said, 'It's an awkward time to start a new school.' But at least she didn't pull the disapproving face.

'I'll manage, miss,' I told her, wanting to get away. A couple of kids from her next class were already lining up outside the door.

She wasn't quite ready to let me go just yet, however, and I wondered whether she was going to ask me about the wallet. I waited for her to find a way of broaching the subject; she must have been curious. But in the end she said, 'I'll double-check your old school has sent everything through.'

'Thanks, miss. I'd appreciate that.'

She nodded and I was at last allowed to join the bustle in the corridors as everyone hurried to their next class.

For me it was English, and I dawdled, going the long way round. I enjoy English more than history – my mum's influence, I'm sure – but I was trying to spot faces in the crowd. I used both of the main block's sets of stairs, walked the length of two corridors, and was disappointed if not surprised that I didn't see who I was looking for. Too many kids at Brook, lots of them with blond or spiky hair.

I wanted to make another circuit, but was going to be the last into English anyway and didn't want to risk being too late. I doubled back on myself and hurried along. I'd have to wait until lunch, search the school from top to bottom if I had to. But it looked like the search had come to me, because Mr Coleburn was waiting impatiently outside the English room. I tried to look shocked when I saw him standing there.

'You, Malarkey. My office. Now!' There were no first names this time around.

The man was seething, his immaculate appearance obviously ruffled. It had taken him only a few minutes to realize what was missing, but even less time to blame me, and I told myself I'd been stupid to expect anything else. Now I was worried.

I wanted to drop the paperweight out of my pocket. I passed at least three litter bins, but Mr Coleburn wasn't letting me out of his sight this time. He followed me. I ignored the looks I got from the other kids – I was getting used to being the centre of attention.

Back behind his desk but standing this time, and without Mr Macallan, he hissed, 'Where are they?' The papers on his desk were scattered and messy, his filing cabinet drawers open.

I shook my head. 'I don't—'

It was as if he was a different man to the one I'd seen earlier; no fake concern, all self-composure had been lost. He was rattled and I realized Dominic Dom must have stolen something important after all.

He slammed his fist down onto his desk, making the remaining paperweights sitting there bounce. I wondered if I could slip the particularly gaudy one I had in my pocket onto his desk if he turned his back.

'I am at the end of my tether with you, boy! I want them back this second. This *very* second. Open your bag!'

I did as I was told, placing it on the chair in front of me. He came round from behind his desk and burrowed through my belongings. The thought did jump into my head that whatever had been in the blue file might actually be in my bag, the same as the wallet had been. But Mr Coleburn's temper rose when he realized that what he was searching for wasn't anywhere among my books and folders. 'What have you got in your pockets?'

I took my mobile out, hoping he didn't ask me to turn out my pockets completely. 'My phone.'

'What else? What else?'

'Cigarettes.' I had to hand them over.

'You shouldn't have them in school,' he said, crushing the pack in his hand, and pointedly ignoring the pained expression on my face – that was my last pack. 'Anything else?'

I patted my pockets as if to prove they were empty,

but in doing so was actually covering the bulge of the paperweight. No way was he getting it back now. An eye for an eye; ten Marlboros for a paperweight. I'd enjoy dropping it from a great height.

But it wasn't the paperweight he was after. 'You have stolen the Year Eleven report cards,' he told me, stabbing a finger at me. 'If you do not return them this instant I give you my word that you will be in the most serious trouble of your life, young man.'

My mind was working quickly; Mr Coleburn had threatened me with a bad report earlier. The cards would have been waiting to be completed by the subject teachers, then counter-signed by the Head of Year, before being given out to the students in registration and taken home at the end of next week. For some it would be a means to parental praise and larger Easter eggs, for others just another slanging match and tears before bed time. But what use would blank report cards be to anyone? And why couldn't Mr Coleburn simply get some more from the stationery cupboard or wherever?

'I want to see your locker,' he snapped. 'Now, boy. *Now*.'

The truth hadn't worked earlier, but I was willing to give it another go. 'When I was waiting for you last lesson, this boy climbed in through the window and took a blue pocket file from out of the filing cabinet.' I didn't have to admit I'd opened the window for him.

Mr Coleburn was halted in his tracks, and looked genuinely confused. 'What?'

'He climbed in through the window, looked through all your papers and things, and—'

Mr Coleburn was shaking his head. 'May I ask why you didn't tell me this earlier?'

'I didn't want to be a grass. I'm trying to make friends, and nobody wants a grasser hanging around with them.' It was half the truth, definitely.

The problem was, I reckoned Mr Coleburn was the type of man to admire grassers. He probably made them prefects, because they reminded him of how he'd been as a youngster. 'You must think I was born yesterday,' he scoffed, the anger returning. 'First you are caught red-handed – *red-handed* – with a member of staff's wallet, and come to me with some half-baked excuse of being given it by two other thieves, and now this. *Now* you claim a cat burglar stole the Year Eleven report cards while you happily watched him do it. According to you, Mr Malarkey, this school must be overrun with villains and thieves.' There were flecks of saliva at the corners of his mouth as he ushered me out into the corridor again. 'I want to see your locker. This very second.' He didn't give me the chance to retrieve my bag.

I was marched in silence to the ground floor of the main block, to the Year Eleven cloakroom. When we got there I went to open my empty locker for him, but he snatched the padlock key from me and did it for himself. He ground his teeth at just how empty it was.

He breathed heavily through his clenched teeth, almost hissing. 'I'd intended to give those report cards to the Year Eleven subject tutors while the students were enjoying tomorrow's football match,' he told me. He'd lowered his voice, but the anger was sharp in his words. 'I *still* intend to do so.' His eyes blazed as they met mine. 'If for any reason I am unable to do this, I guarantee you here and now that your time at Brook High will be over. I also give you my word that I will make it extremely difficult for you to find another school willing to take you in time to sit your GCSEs in June.' A vein throbbed in his forehead. 'Do I make myself perfectly clear?'

I nodded slowly. Claiming innocence yet again at this point would be worthless.

He held my eyes for a good ten seconds. 'Think about your position very carefully, Mr Malarkey.' He turned and stalked away back towards Top Block. 'Your bag will be returned to you after I have searched it thoroughly,' he told me without looking round.

I watched him go, and tried to take stock of my thoughts. I wanted to follow the threads and work out what had happened. This was the way I saw things:

The girl with the perfect beauty spot knew my name and pointed me out to Blondie and Spike, who stole my bag. Then I have my bag returned complete with Mr Macallan's wallet tucked inside. I'm accused of the theft, taken to Mr Coleburn's office, where while I wait Dominic Dom (who's got the same taste in trainers) climbs in through the window and steals the report cards. I then take the blame for that as well.

Yet it was this second theft which seemed far more important – enough to make the Head of Year lose his rag. I realized that he hadn't particularly cared about the wallet; a petty misdemeanour, that was all. He hadn't even mentioned it just now, and his lack of interest in the childish theft had been reflected in his attitude towards me at the time. The report cards, however . . .

I wondered if stealing the report cards had been the intention all along. I wondered if the wallet was simply a way of getting me into that office at the right time –

the specific time – so I could let the real thief in. Was it some kind of elaborate set-up by Blondie and Spike? And if it was, then maybe I wasn't a thread in this spider's web after all. Maybe I was the fly.

BAD DAY AT BROOK HIGH

FOUR

If you were able to look down on the school buildings from a plane you'd see they make a broken yet still distinct capital 'E' and capital 'H'. As in the word/sound associated with confusion and exasperation – 'EH?' As in 'WHAT THE HELL?' As in 'I HAVEN'T GOT THE FOGGIEST WHAT YOU'RE ON ABOUT!' It's the expression most kids use at least once a day during some incomprehensible lesson or other, and therefore, I think, kind of fitting.

The long back and bottom of the 'E' shape is the main block, with its four floors made up of classrooms, cloakrooms and the library; while Top Block sits – surprise, surprise – at the top. The middle bar of the 'E' is slightly adrift from the rest and is the school's main entrance foyer, with the secretary's office below and the staff room and Head's office above (Mr Springbank is the Head – a short, hunched man I've only ever seen from a distance). The 'H' shape across the way is the science block, the technology block, the main dining hall and the sixth-form common room, all connected by narrow paths. The gym block is a lonely island of brawn over brain behind the 'E', with the tennis courts in between and the playing fields beyond. Scattered around here, there and everywhere are mobile classrooms of both the garden-shed and biscuit-tin variety.

Brook High is a big school that has grown bigger over the years. And it should have sprawled, but because it's ringed by busy roads and a housing estate it has become packed in tight. The playing field had once curled around the main block with room enough for another football pitch, while nowadays it is simply an extension of the teachers' car park.

Yes, Brook's a big school, with lots of places to get lost, and maybe even a few to hide. Which was going to make it difficult for me.

I didn't know what to do with the paperweight; felt resentful enough towards Mr Coleburn that I didn't want to give it back, but was reluctant to simply throw it away. I ended up leaving it in my locker because I didn't want to be caught with it on me. I'd decide what to do with it later.

There was no point in going to English – not without my bag, my books. I doubted I'd be going to any of the afternoon's lessons either, because I didn't want to be anywhere Mr Macallan or Mr Coleburn could easily find me. I decided to keep moving, reasoning that if a teacher saw me hanging around they'd be more likely to ask questions.

There were classroom murmurings on either side: the droning voice of a kid forced to read out loud, the waning enthusiasm of a teacher, the buzz of a disrupted lesson. The school felt calm and quiet, and even in trainers my footsteps seemed far too loud. I wasn't fooled, however. Brook isn't a calm or quiet school by any stretch of the imagination. What school is? But there was more to Brook, because something was happening here – something in between the lessons, something behind the teachers' backs.

As a smoker I have access to people and places other

kids might not. I get to see the nooks and crannies which are out of sight of the staff room; I get to mingle in the quiet corners with the real eyes and ears of the school. In my experience it's not just smokers who need a hidey-hole, but those who tend to stretch and flout the rules in other ways too. Those who practise a far wider delinquency often use a cigarette as a mere smokescreen – no pun intended.

I knew what I had to do. I had to find Blondie and Spike, or Dominic Dom. The girl with the perfect beauty spot seemed less important now – to be honest she could have been anybody who simply shared a class with me, and therefore completely unconnected. No, it was the lads I was after. I needed them if I was going to prove my innocence. And maybe I knew a place to start looking.

I headed outside, and at last the sun was making an appearance. It wasn't warm or even particularly bright, but at least it was having a go. I wandered the school's edges. I avoided the Quad – the flagstone square in between the 'E' and the 'H', a crossroads for most of the paths between the blocks which all windows seemed to stare out onto – but I still managed to bump into a couple of teachers. Only one asked me where I was going, and I kept moving as I said over my shoulder, 'I've got a message for Mr Coleburn, sir.'

Through a fire door around the back of the drama hall there's a narrow passage between the grey brick of the school and the high fences of the neighbouring gardens, where muddy footprints and crushed Benson and Hedges proved that even today's bad weather hadn't stopped this from being one of the more favoured smokers' lairs. It was sheltered from the wind; maybe from much of the rain as well thanks to the trees that overhung from the gardens. A skinny fair-haired girl without a coat was leaning up against the wall and dragging what warmth she could out of her cigarette. She had the sleeves of her school jumper pulled down over her hands, her shoulders hunched against the chilly breeze. I thought I recognized her from one of my classes but couldn't be sure. Her sharp eyes weighed me up as I leaned on the fence opposite and searched my pockets one by one for the Marlboro Lights I knew I didn't have. And when I didn't find them I swore quietly under my breath.

'Don't suppose I could scrounge a fag off you, could I?' I asked.

'Last one,' she told me. She watched me carefully.

I nodded, stuffed my hands in my pockets. I knew she was watching me but wouldn't meet her gaze. I read the graffiti on the drama hall wall: 'THE TAILORS' written in red, 'TAILOR-MADE' in black. I'd come here for a quick smoke a couple of times since I'd been at Brook and had never bothered about it before – it didn't mean anything to me – but now I was on the lookout for *anything* that might mean *something*. I filed it away at the back of my mind. Somebody else had written 'MR COLEBURN'S A NOB-HEAD', which only proved the teachers rarely made an appearance here, because otherwise it would certainly have been scrubbed off long ago.

'Is this where everybody comes?' I asked the girl.

She shrugged one of her shoulders.

'I'm new,' I said.

She nodded. She knew. Of course she did. Who didn't?

'So do you know anybody who could sell me some fags? Mr Coleburn confiscated my last pack.' I nodded at the graffiti. 'And he's a nob-head.'

She smiled at this, despite herself. 'The tuck shop,' she told me.

'The tuck shop? They sell cigarettes?' I couldn't help sounding surprised. 'Do the teachers—?'

She laughed at me. 'The teachers don't do nothing,' she said. I would have pressed her further but she took one last drag on her cigarette and offered me the remainder. Which I took with a smile of thanks. 'I'm meant to be at the toilet,' she said, and hurried away back towards the fire exit into the main block, to return to whichever lesson she'd snuck out of.

I watched her go, mulling over what she'd said, wondering if the tuck shop would be open this lunch time. And then I considered the cigarette between my fingers.

I was tempted, and I still felt like I needed one, and I knew my mum would never find out. But . . .

I let it burn all the way down to the filter. And I didn't even feel brave or pleased with myself or stronger as a person for resisting temptation; I just felt like I could do with a smoke.

At 12.15 the lunch-time bell finally rang, and within seconds kids were appearing around the back of the drama hall and lighting up. It suddenly got crowded. I knew I was a bit out of place standing by myself, not smoking, and was on the receiving end of a few unfriendly glares. But I hung around for a few minutes, watching the faces, not recognizing any, and soon realized that most of those here were Brook's 'wannabe rebels'. They advertised the fact by swearing loudly and wearing obscure band T-shirts underneath their uniforms. They were the trendy waywards; I didn't think they were Blondie and Spike's type. The type of kids I was chasing would be the truly mutinous ones, who saw it as more of a career than a fashion statement. Maybe the type who sold ciggies from the school tuck shop?

I slipped away as casually as possible.

Room 38 was one of the garden-shed variety of mobile classrooms close to the main block and doubled as the tuck shop most lunch times. You had to queue up outside – even if it was raining, snowing, hailstoning – and got served through an open window. It was supposedly run by students studying Business and Finance for GCSE as part of their coursework, but I'd noticed that those clever Year Elevens often hired/bribed younger kids to suffer the menial duties of customer service while they sat playing cards at a table in the warm and dry. And today proved no different.

The spotty, floppy-haired boy serving at the chilly open window was maybe Year Eight, while three older lads sat around chatting and laughing in the background. None of them were Blondie or Spike. I waited my turn patiently, listening in case anyone in front of me was asking for something other than M&Ms and a can of Coke. When it was my turn I said loud enough for *everyone* to hear, 'Mars Bar, Quavers and a packet of fags.'

The Year Eight looked suddenly fidgety, and one of the older lads was on his feet, pushing the younger kid aside. He leaned out of the window at me, his shoulders filling the window, staring at me nastily with little piggy eyes. 'I'd ask nicely if I was you,' he warned me. 'Or all you'll be getting is a slap.' He didn't look like your stereotypical Business and Finance student.

We locked eyes. But I repeated my order quietly, adding 'please' at the end.

He never took his squinty little gaze off me. I wondered if he knew who I was like everybody else seemed to. Over his shoulder I could see his two mates watching me carefully. 'Thirty p each,' he told me. 'Three for a quid.' He laughed at how funny he thought he was.

'Almost reasonable,' I said. 'But I'll just have two.'

He handed them over. 'D'you want anything else?' he asked.

'Mars Bar,' I reminded him.

'Anything else?'

'Quavers.'

I was annoying him. 'Anything *else*, I said.'

'What've you got?'

'What d'you want?'

I shrugged. 'What've you got?'

He curled his lip at me. 'You're getting on my nerves.'

'No, honest,' I said. 'I don't know what *else* you sell. What *else* have you got?'

'Tell him to piss off,' one of his mates shouted from inside the hut.

'I'm going to,' he replied.

'So hurry up and do it. Tell him: Piss off, Malarkey. We don't like new kids around here.'

I heard the harsh laughter from inside and held up

my hands. 'No worries, I'm going. Okay?' I paid the Year Eight kid and retreated quickly with my chocolate, crisps and cigarettes. 'See? I'm gone.' All I wanted was for somebody to not know my name around here.

FIVE

The butch dinner lady standing guard at the dining hall looked suspicious for a second or two and blocked me like a well-practised rugby player. Each year had a designated time to eat, with Year Eleven being on third sitting today. I held my Mars Bar and Quavers up for her to see. 'Packed lunch,' I said. Then added with a guilty shrug, 'I ate my sandwiches at break.' She didn't look happy about it, but let me through all the same. Then watched to make sure I didn't queue for a hot meal.

I took a table towards the back of the hall near the cutlery trays and paid close attention to the faces at the rest of tables. I reckoned that if there was anywhere to find nine out of ten kids at lunch time it was going to be the dining hall. So if my luck was in, I might just find those faces I was looking for.

Unfortunately, as I watched the lines of hungry students lengthen, and the noise level quickly became loud enough to blur out all but the closest conversations, I realized how difficult finding one or two among this crowd was going to be. I hung on though, because there wasn't much else I could do. I ate my crisps slowly.

The sudden spit of static as the Tannoy system was switched on startled me. I'd heard it used before on several occasions – members of staff were forever being called away to the office, or the caretaker was being sent to deal with some problem or other. Not that the teachers were particularly fond of it, and I'd even seen Miss Walker trying to muffle the speaker in her room with a scarf when it was used maybe half a dozen times during one of her lessons. My old school hadn't had the luxury of a Tannoy, however, so I was still in the habit of jumping whenever it crackled into life. And right now it had my full attention as Mr Coleburn's voice boomed out of it.

I saw several faces in the hall look up to one of the two speakers high on the wall at either end of the dining hall, and couldn't help looking up at one myself. The hall didn't go completely quiet, but the noise level lessened as people paused to listen.

'This is an announcement for John Malarkey of Eleven C. Would John Malarkey of Eleven C come to Mr Coleburn's office immediately.'

I waited anxiously to see if he was going to say anything else, like an offer of a reward for bringing me in dead or alive, but there was only a second static pop as the system was switched off. Still, half of me expected a Mexican wave of heads turning from the speakers towards where I was sitting. Thankfully it never came. Most people seemed to go straight back to their food, the conversation returning to shouts across the tables.

Maybe there were one or two who glanced at me, I couldn't tell for sure. Maybe there were one or two nudges and nods in my direction. And I was tempted to leave. But thought, if I did, it might make it far too obvious that, yes, I was Malarkey of 11C.

So I stayed put. And ignoring the needling paranoia at the back of my mind, I redoubled my efforts at trying to find Blondie or Spike in the crowd. The sooner the better, that was for sure.

Twice I thought I spotted Spike; both times it was

just another lad with a similar haircut. The fact that most of the kids wore uniform didn't help. And then I spotted a pair of trainers . . .

It wasn't Blondie or Spike, or even the report card thief. He wore glasses, and was a bit too long-limbed and scrawny looking for his own good. He had so much gel in his short dark hair it had a plastic sheen. He was in uniform as well – he could have been one of a hundred, but he was wearing black Adidas trainers. The same as Blondie and Spike, only two of the stripes remained white; the third had been coloured in black.

I watched him carry his tray to an empty table two or three rows across the hall from me, and noticed that no one went to sit with him at first. Even though I reckoned he was too gangly to appear intimidating in any way, other kids squeezed themselves onto already full tables rather than share with him. And when somebody eventually did join him, this second lad wore Adidas as well. I was interested to notice that the newcomer had blacked out *two* of his three stripes – very interested indeed. And I realized I shouldn't have been looking for faces in the crowd after all, because at Brook it was obviously the footwear that mattered.

I wondered what kind of trainers the older kids at the tuck shop had been wearing, and kicked myself for not thinking of checking.

The second lad was shorter, stockier, and if not exactly fat, undoubtedly greedy. I watched as he stuffed away what could easily have been a double portion. He did most of the talking too, which would have offended my mother who's forever telling me, 'Not with your mouth full, Johnny.' He gesticulated a lot with his cutlery, pointing with his knife, waving his fork, and his skinny friend nodded at everything he said. It crossed my mind to go sit with them – just stroll right up and introduce myself. But I reckoned they'd probably know who I was anyway, and I certainly didn't want to bring too much attention to myself after Mr Coleburn's Tannoy announcement. So I waited until the bigger kid had polished off his meal and when the two got up to leave I followed.

They headed outside into the crowded Quad. Other kids avoided them, stepping out of their way, even leaving the path and braving the sodden, muddy verges to steer clear of them – or their trainers. I followed only a few steps behind. I managed to get close enough to hear Slim call the bigger kid George, if not to discover exactly what their conversation was about.

Once inside the main block they split up. Big George disappeared up the stairs while Slim looked as though he was either heading for Top Block or the Year Ten cloakrooms. I chose to stick with Slim, reckoning he was easier to spot above the rest of the heads in the packed corridor. But that was a mistake. Because before I could find out exactly where he was going, Mr Macallan was suddenly bearing down on me.

The last thing I wanted was to end up back in Mr Coleburn's office with the two teachers playing 'bad cop, worse cop'. Once they'd got me trapped in there I doubted they'd ever let me out again, and I didn't think it would take them too long to decide to call the police when I was still unable to return Mr Macallan's property. So if I was going to find out what was happening here, if I was going to prove my innocence, I had to keep well out of their way.

The maths teacher hadn't spotted me yet — I was buried in amongst the other uniforms. I quickly tried the handle of the nearest classroom door only to find it locked. All I could do was turn round and walk back the way I'd come, cursing my luck for losing sight of Slim.

I could hear the teacher behind me as he waded through the packs of students, huffing and snapping at anyone on the verge of some misdemeanour or other. I attached myself to a group of four lads, hoping I'd appear to be one of their friends. I knew that all Mr Macallan had to do was stop bothering with the kids around him and lift his gaze a few metres further along the corridor to be able to see me. I hoped the back of my head looked the same as everybody else's.

I was keeping pace and sticking close to the four lads, and they were chatting happily enough between themselves, taking little notice of me. But the maths teacher was getting closer; he'd be sure to notice me if I made a sudden run for it now. I could see the door that led outside onto the Quad at the end of the corridor.

I jabbed the lad nearest to me with my elbow. 'Hey, mate?'

He turned to look at me, frowning, probably noticing me for the first time.

I smiled, and stuck my foot out.

He didn't see it coming. He kicked my shin, made an 'Urgh' sound as he stumbled, and then went down. As he fell he shot out a hand to save himself, grabbed his pal's jacket, and instead of regaining his balance pulled him down as well.

The two curled into a heap on the floor. Their friends stopped to see what was happening and, as friends tend to do, started laughing. Other kids gathered round, wanting to join in with whatever was so funny.

'What's going on there?' Mr Macallan bellowed. 'Get up, laddie! What on earth do you think you're playing at?' He stormed up to take control of a situation which really didn't need his intervention. But he was a teacher, and it's probably what he thought he got paid for. 'On your feet!'

Meanwhile I was at the end of the corridor, through the door and outside – out of sight.

I didn't hang around in the Quad but kept moving. Not that I was too sure where I should be going. I wandered aimlessly, staring at people's feet. The close call with Mr Macallan had left me with an eye aimed over my shoulder, and I guessed keeping on the move was the wisest idea. A moving target was harder to hit – that was my thinking.

I was tempted to go back to the tuck shop, but was wary of pushing my luck. Instead I made a luckless circuit around the blocks. There wasn't a single face I recognized; nobody else was wearing black Adidas. How could I be sure it was just black? Should I follow *anybody* in Adidas, whatever the colour? I was checking out the bike sheds when the Head of Year's voice once again boomed out of the Tannoy. 'This is the second announcement for John Malarkey of Eleven C. Would John Malarkey of Eleven C come to collect his belongings from Mr Coleburn's office as soon as possible.' It echoed across the whole of the school.

If the dining hall paranoia had been needles, it was knives now. I stared at my own feet, wary of meeting anybody's eyes. It was a clever ploy by the Head of Year to make it sound as if I wasn't in trouble any more, saying he simply wanted me to collect my bag, but I wasn't falling for it. I needed to get out of sight of as many people as possible, and reckoned the best place to do it would be the smokers' lair behind the drama hall.

At least I had a couple of cigarettes with me this time and wouldn't look so out of place, but when I stepped out of the fire door I was more than a little surprised to realize I'd joined the back of a queue. There had to be two dozen or more kids all waiting in line, squeezed in between the drama hall and the neighbouring fences, everybody a bit nervous and fidgety.

I tried to peer over some heads to see what we were all waiting for. 'Stop pushing,' the girl in front protested as I leaned past her. She shoved me back with the flat of her hand on my chest. 'They said they've got enough for everyone.' She was as tall as I was, lots of curly red hair and a cigarette on the go.

I nodded. 'Yeah, sorry,' I said. 'I just wasn't sure if this was the right place or not.'

'Where else would it be?' she said, turning her back on me again.

I almost said the tuck shop, but stayed quiet. A lad who'd got what he wanted from the top of the line scuttled past clutching whatever it was to his chest. I was only one of many who tried to get a closer look; some hands even made a grab at him. He shook them off angrily, squeezing by us all. It had looked like a letter or something to me. He disappeared round the corner and the queue moved up a step or two.

I tapped the girl on the shoulder. 'I only just heard about it,' I said. I tried to look dumb. 'What, you know . . . ? What do I . . . ?' I let the question hang, hoping she'd follow it up herself.

She frowned at me, blew smoke. 'Ten quid,' she told me. 'It's always been ten quid.'

I grinned at her, mopping my brow to over-exaggerate my relief. 'Somebody told me they were going to charge fifteen,' I lied.

She suddenly looked worried and nudged the girl in front of her. 'He reckons it's fifteen quid, not ten,' she whispered. And the looks on the faces in the queue grew even more anxious and nervy.

'I haven't got fifteen,' a lad four or five places in front whined. 'Shit! Can somebody lend us a fiver?'

The line began to break down and dissolve, and as it did I caught a glimpse of what was happening at the top end. It was Slim from the dining hall, and I was sure he was holding the blue pocket file that had been stolen right before my very eyes from the Head of Year's desk. He was selling the report cards. The report cards for which I was taking the blame. I watched as he snatched some money from a kid with glasses and handed him the stiff white A4 sheet.

I realized instantly that I had no hope of returning them to Mr Coleburn now – even less hope of clearing my name. And to be honest, it *really* pissed me off!

I nudged the girl in front of me again. 'Someone told me they were fakes anyway,' I said, nodding seriously. 'Just photocopies.'

I left her to pass that message on to the already agitated queue and followed the kid with glasses as he hurried past me, folding the report card carefully and putting it into his bag.

He was wearing clumpy school shoes which probably reflected his mother's taste rather than his own. He made his way to the Year Eleven cloakroom and put his bag with the report card tucked inside into his locker.

'Are they worth the money?' I asked him over his shoulder.

He slammed his locker shut and spun round on the spot. 'What? What're you on about?' He was blond, pale and scared, overly defensive – he didn't look like your perennial offender type to me. His uniform was exactly as the school rules said it should be, crisp and clean too, but the lenses of his glasses needed cleaning. The first thing he did was glance down at my trainers. He seemed a little mollified by my Converse. 'Who're you?'

At last, I'd found somebody who didn't already know me! It made me want to be his best friend!

'I need one too,' I whispered, making out I was as worried and nervous as he was. 'But someone told me they're fakes.'

'No, no, they're real.' He shook his head vigorously. 'They're all signed and everything.'

'They're already signed? Are you sure?'

He didn't seem to notice the real surprise in my voice. 'Well, yeah, of course. There'd be no point if they weren't, would there?'

Jigsaw pieces fell into place. Somehow someone (who wore black Adidas trainers, no doubt) had discovered that Mr Coleburn had pre-signed the Year Eleven report cards, and decided they could make a tidy profit with them.

There were several kids milling around the cloakroom and corridor, and I was ever conscious of being recognized, but I needed more information. 'I'm John, by the way,' I said conspiratorially. He wasn't going to tell me his name and I shrugged to show it didn't bother me. I could see it was printed on the front of his locker anyway: SIMON PENN, 11B. 'It's just what I heard,' I said. 'But the word going around is that they're fakes.'

He didn't trust me (I didn't blame him) but he took his bag out of his locker again, and keeping a wary eye on the other kids he unzipped it to look inside. We huddled against the locker with our backs to the corridor as we checked to make sure it was real. Which it obviously was. Printed at the top was the Brook High insignia and the words 'YEAR 11 REPORT CARD', then the card was separated into two columns – small boxes on one side for the subject name, large rectangles on the other for the teachers to make their comments. At the bottom was the Head of Year's bold and looping signature in blue ink, dated for next Friday, the day they'd be handed out in registration.

It was no wonder Mr Coleburn had been about ready to burst at the seams, because he was sure to get his knuckles rapped plenty hard for signing them up front, without even bothering to see how well the students in his care were coping. He'd given them carte blanche to write their own reports. All anybody had to do was get a couple of friends with different handwriting to fill in the teachers' comments and they'd be laughing. And when you looked at it like that, a tenner was a more than reasonable price for most kids.

I'd seen easily a couple of dozen kids queuing, which was £240 right there. But I knew there were nearly three hundred of us in Year Eleven. If only a third or a half wanted to buy, it was still a very tidy profit.

Stealing them was a nicely executed operation too – you had to admire the organizational skills involved. One lad to do the actual thieving, another to do the selling, then a third to take the blame. And if I hadn't been that third, I might have admitted to feeling impressed.

'See, it's fine, yeah?' Simon said, looking to me for confirmation.

'It's perfect,' I told him.

He was quick to shove his bag back inside his locker, his relief plain to see.

'You don't really look like the type who needs one, Simon.'

'What?'

'The report card. You don't look like someone the teachers usually need to give a hard time to.'

He wasn't saying anything.

I made sure nobody was taking any notice of us, nobody within earshot. 'It's true, isn't it?' I pushed. 'You're no teacher's pet or anything, you don't kiss arse, but you're not a troublemaker and you're certainly not thick.' I was guessing, but it was an educated guess, mixed with a touch of compliment. 'You've always had decent enough reports before, so what's wrong now?' And I could see by his face that I was hitting the mark. Still, he wasn't going to admit to anything just yet.

'Listen, Simon, I'm new here,' I confided. 'And believe me when I say I'm finding it tough to find my way around. I'm getting a whole heap of grief from kids wearing black Adidas trainers; they really seem to have it in for me. Have they got it in for you too?'

He shrugged, but his cheeks had darkened. It wasn't a blush exactly, it was angrier than that. He leaned forward to whisper, 'I'm in the Homework Club.'

This meant nothing to me. I shrugged to prove it.

'I can't get out of it,' he said desperately. 'The Tailors have—'

'The Tailors?' I remembered the graffiti from round the back of the drama hall.

He flinched when I said it so loud. His eyes were scanning faces and feet again.

'Come on,' I said. 'Let's go somewhere we can talk.'

Simon was reluctant. He shook his head.

I was about to push him some more – I needed to know what he knew – but a roar from the opposite end of the corridor stopped me in my tracks.

'*John Malarkey!*' Mr Macallan bellowed. 'I want a word with *you*, laddie!'

'I really need to talk,' I told Simon urgently. 'I'll come find you, okay?' He tried to squirm away from me but I grabbed his arm. '*Okay?*' I insisted. And only when he nodded did I let him go.

Then I was away.

Six

'Malarkey!'

There was a group of kids coming inside while I was trying to get out, and they didn't like my hurry or my elbows, but I guessed the look on my face stopped them from fighting back too hard. Even so, I suffered a face full of grubby anorak, kicked shins and trampled toes. I plunged through the door and left them to block the maths teacher's way as I ducked down the side of the tennis courts.

'MALARKEY!'

But I was gone.

That growing feeling of being a marked man made me want to get off school grounds as quickly as possible. I weaved my way between mobile classrooms and bike sheds, not wanting to draw attention to myself by running but not exactly dawdling either. My watch told me there was only a quarter of an hour or so to go before the end of lunch, which was why the two bouncer-like, duffel-coated dinner ladies at the school gates cast me a baleful eye as I walked out onto Raymond Avenue. There was a steady trickle of students heading back for the afternoon's lessons and I walked against the flow.

It wasn't a wide street; the parked cars were boot-to-bonnet on either side and the houses only had scrappy little gardens out front (no room for trees), and yet I noticed the way it felt like a weight of claustrophobia had been lifted from my shoulders. It surprised me how much easier I breathed – as if I'd been a beetle in a box while inside Brook's grey walls, and nobody had bothered to punch any air holes in the lid.

I had to stop and give myself a second or two to lean back against somebody's garden wall. Slowly I took, and held, a shuddery breath. My mind was catching up with me. Exactly what was happening here, now, was finally settling into place. I was up to my neck in trouble. And I was big enough to admit it scared me!

I took another long breath, holding it until my head cleared.

I'd run away, when maybe I should have just taken Mr Macallan by the hand and led him round the back of the drama hall so he could see what was what with his own eyes. But that wouldn't have necessarily proved I hadn't stolen the report cards – or his wallet. I should have gone straight to Mr Coleburn; I should have stuck to my story, made him believe me. I was making myself look guiltier and guiltier by always running away.

I hated running away. Should I go back?

I stared hard at the big ugly school, imagining the stale air that filled the corridors had left a nasty taste in my mouth. I couldn't face going back, not yet. Neither could I shake the feeling that some invisible net was closing in on me, and told myself it was best to jump through the holes while they were still wide enough and I still had the chance.

But what was to stop the teachers from getting the police involved? If I wasn't able to prove my innocence to Mr Macallan I knew I wouldn't stand a chance with the coppers. Although when I thought about it, about what Mr Coleburn had said, I reckoned he'd actually given me a deadline and an ultimatum. He'd said he wanted to give the report cards to the other teachers tomorrow afternoon. That was the ultimatum he'd given me. That was my deadline.

Perhaps he was running scared himself? Because of how bad it would look to parents if they knew he'd signed the reports without giving a damn what was going to be written on them. The rest of the teachers obviously knew what he did – they must have seen it plenty of times before – but if the parents, the PTA, the board of governors found out, wouldn't questions be asked and complaints be made? I didn't doubt it for a second.

It meant he'd also want to keep a rein on Mr Macallan, as far as he could. 'Come now, what does a video card really matter?' was what he'd say. If the maths teacher took things further, then the Head of Year would be forced to as well, and I believed absolutely that Mr Coleburn wanted a lid keeping on things just now.

I went over what Mr Coleburn had said one more time, and was confident now that I had until tomorrow afternoon, until this football match he and Miss Walker had talked about. I realized I didn't even know what football match it was, and wondered whether this could be the reason why Blondie and Spike and their cronies had singled me out. I wasn't just the new kid; I was also the one who didn't join in, who hadn't mixed. I knew I was only at Brook for a couple of months, so why bother? I'd take my exams and go – no looking back. I hadn't made any effort whatsoever to be a part of the school. I had no friends, no allies, no one to defend me. It made me an easy target.

But it was no use complaining about it now. Whatever the reason, I had just over twenty-four hours to prove my innocence or I was going to get kicked out of the school and have to wave those exams goodbye.

So what now?

Good question.

I had two plans. The first was to hang around at the end of school in the hope of catching Simon Penn. And I knew it wasn't much of a hope, so my second idea was to have a snoop around the gym block. I was curious as to why Blondie and Spike had taken my bag there. Could it be a meeting place for their gang?

Because it *was* a gang – had to be. The trainers were proof enough, while everybody wearing them was too well organized not to be part of something bigger. Which also meant they had to have a leader. Somebody somewhere had to have the brains, and the balls. And it was the leader I wanted.

They'd made it personal, plucked me from the crowd, picked on me to take the fall. I wanted to prove just how personal *I* could get.

If I wasn't going to lessons this afternoon the most sensible thing would be to get out of sight of the school. There were some shops a couple of streets over where I could bide my time while I figured out which of my two plans was the wisest course of action. Although I had to admit, either/or, they both sounded a bit too much like clutching at straws.

There was a chippy, a grocer's-cum-newsagent, a beer-off, a chemist and a hairdresser's on the corner of Dean Street and Henning Street. It looked as though they'd been specifically planned when the estate was built. There were half a dozen parking spaces, a telephone box, a postbox and a bus shelter. The stiff breeze blew sweet wrappers, crisp packets and chip papers across on the pavement, trapped them at the base of walls, or tumbled them along the gutter. It was proof enough that many of the kids had spent their lunch hour here; almost as obvious as signing the chip shop wall 'BROOK HIGH WOZ 'ERE!' A few were still hanging around, kicking their heels, seemingly unconcerned about being late back. They were gathered around their cigarettes in the bus shelter or under the newsagent's awning.

As I walked up I was checking out their trainers — this before I even bothered to look at their faces. 'Bingo,' I whispered to myself when I spotted a pair of my favourite brand.

He had a single stripe blacked out. He was large-framed, broad-shouldered, with a head shaped almost like a bullet, but much bigger — so more like an artillery shell fired from a tank. His denim jacket was too small for him, looking as though he wouldn't be able to do up the buttons if he tried. He was taking money from a younger kid in a green cagoule who wasn't part of the gang, giving him something in return. I walked over with my friendliest grin. The younger kid disappeared quickly, and for some reason I couldn't fathom was blushing furiously, as though he'd been caught in his sister's underwear drawer.

The lad with the weird-shaped head gave me the once over. 'Yeah? What?'

I think that's what he said. He didn't actually move his lips and the words were little more than grunts.

'I want the same as him,' I said, hooking my thumb at the embarrassed lad hurrying across the road, heading back in the direction of the school.

'Grunt–grunt.'

I cocked my ear towards him. 'I do beg your pardon. Could you repeat that?'

My sarcasm tickled his ear lighter than a feather. 'Five quid.' He held out a folded piece of paper.

I whistled through my teeth. 'That's a bit steep, isn't it? I mean, is it worth it?'

He shoved the paper into his left breast pocket, then took a second folded piece out of his right pocket. 'Two quid.'

'Seems fairer,' I said, not knowing what was going on but rolling with it anyway.

We exchanged and I unfolded the scrap of paper to find the number '574.1' written in red pen. He was watching me, and although I didn't have a clue what it was for, or what it meant, I smiled and said thanks. He nodded gruffly, then walked away, also heading back in the direction of Brook.

I watched him go, pondering the number, thinking I'd been ripped off. I wondered how big a number I would have got for a fiver. And then I began to wonder how many people were actually in this gang.

I knew of Blondie and Spike, the bag snatchers; Dominic Dom the thief; Slim the seller; Big George (not sure what he did); and the Grunter who grunted. I guessed I really should include the three from the tuck shop too. But who was the leader? Could he be called 'Tailor' by any chance?

*   *   *

I was hungry: the Mars Bar and Quavers hadn't particularly filled me up. I considered an apple or banana or something from the newsagent/grocer's, but knew all I'd be getting for tea from Mum was rabbit food masquerading as healthy vegetarian cuisine – so fish, chips and mushy peas it was, then.

It wasn't until I was inside the chip shop being served that I noticed the two girls in the bus shelter, and that one of them was watching me. She turned away the second our eyes met, but I'd already seen the perfect beauty spot on her right cheek.

I took my tray of chips over to the bus shelter. The smattering of graffiti on the glass sides was mostly boring tags, no mention of the Tailors. The three lads shuffling their feet with hands stuffed in pockets and up-turned collars weren't wearing Adidas and they mooched away as soon as they'd finished their cigarettes. There were half a dozen orange plastic fold-down seats, one of which was broken, snapped off, and I made myself comfortable next to the girl with the perfect beauty spot. Both she and her friend were pretending to ignore me.

I ate my chips slowly; they were very hot. I realized I'd killed the conversation the two girls had been having and the silence was an awkward one. The friend was tall, stick-thin, with bad hair and a worse complexion. She looked uncomfortable with me being there. She took out a cigarette and lit it quickly.

I blew the steam from my chips and popped a couple more into my mouth. 'Hmmm,' I said, rolling my eyes. 'These're *good*.'

The girl with the beauty spot was staring at me openly now.

I held the tray out to her. 'Want one?'

She looked my grubby school uniform up and down with a wrinkled nose. 'Do I know you?' she asked, but didn't do a very convincing job of making it sound like a question.

I chuckled to myself with a hot chip on my tongue. 'I reckon you do, yes.'

'Oh, I know!' she said, her surprise sounding every bit as authentic as a £6 note. 'You're that boy in my English class. *James* Malarkey.'

I let my chuckle spread across my face in a wide grin. 'Close,' I told her.

She stood up, maybe to look at me better, maybe to put a bit of extra distance between us, and I suddenly realized she was wearing Adidas trainers. I hadn't noticed before because they were sky-blue, and a canvassy type of material rather than the black leather the gang wore. I remembered wondering how much the colour mattered – were female members of this gang able to be a little more fashion conscious? Were girls even allowed to join? She hadn't coloured in any of her stripes.

'That's where you know me from, is it?' I asked. 'English?'

Her eyes were the same colour as her trainers. She gave me a slight, knowing smile, which only moved the right-hand corner of her lips, but lifted her beauty spot a touch higher up her cheek. I decided it was real, not make-up. She flicked her dark hair from off her shoulder as if it irritated her and nodded. 'But you weren't there today, were you?'

I shook my head. 'Otherwise engaged,' I said, thinking about Mr Coleburn stopping me right outside the door to the English lesson.

'Mrs Lang asked where you were, and I had to tell her I'd seen you earlier. I'm sorry. I hope I didn't get you into trouble. Was that why Mr Coleburn was calling for you over the Tannoy earlier?'

'Maybe.' I chewed on a chip thoughtfully. 'Is somebody going to grass you up when you're late back this afternoon?'

'We've got the afternoon off,' she told me. 'Dentist appointment.' She turned to her friend, who nodded.

'Great,' I grinned. 'I've got the afternoon off too.' I looked beyond her to her friend. 'Want to do something fun?'

The friend stamped on her half-finished cigarette. She was wearing black DM shoes. 'Come on, Becky. Let's go.'

'Hey, Becky, now I know your name too,' I beamed.

'So?' Becky sneered.

'So I also know who to tell the teachers is skipping lessons.'

'You think you're clever, don't you?'

I nodded. 'Yep.' I'd had enough of my greasy chips already and stood up to dump them in the litter bin.

She considered me carefully. 'What do you want? Do you want me to say I'm sorry or something?'

I took out one of the cigarettes I'd bought from the tuck shop (force of habit after eating) but didn't light it. 'Sorry for what?'

'For telling those boys who you were. Have you got your bag back?'

I made a show of looking around. 'Can't see it anywhere.'

She shrugged. 'So I'm sorry, okay?' I couldn't tell if she meant it or not.

'What did they say to you?' I asked.

'They just wanted to know who the new kid was.'

'Do you know them?'

'I used to think Drew was really nice.'

'Drew? Is he Blondie or Spike?'

She frowned at this, but was quick to cotton on. 'Oh, he's got dark hair. Drew Buchanan. I thought he was cute back in Year Nine.'

I nodded. Spike was Drew Buchanan. Drew Buchanan had stood over me with his foot raised. 'And do you still think he's cute?'

'He's got an attitude problem.'

I had to laugh. 'No shit.'

She smiled, openly this time. But her friend said, 'Are you coming, Becky?'

Becky shushed her. 'I'm enjoying myself,' she said. Then to me: 'I might decide to like you.'

'As long as it doesn't mean introducing me to any more lads you used to find "cute".'

She held her face down and looked at me through her long, long eyelashes. 'Does this mean you forgive me?'

'Of course,' I lied.

She smiled; I smiled.

'Are you going to smoke that?' she asked.

I was rolling the cigarette around in my fingers. I considered lighting it for a second, but then: 'I'm giving up,' I said.

'Good. I don't like people who smoke,' Becky told me.

'I'll have it,' her friend said quickly, seeming not to care whether she was liked or not.

I handed it over with a smile. Then took the second one out so I could play with that instead. 'But there's still something I don't get,' I said.

Becky looked interested. 'What's that?'

'Your trainers,' I said, pointing down at them. 'So far at Brook I've not met one person I like who wears Adidas.'

She curled her lip. 'That's just some of the boys playing games and thinking they're clever.' She gave a dismissive waft of her hand. 'It's their *gang thing*.' She sounded like it was the most childish thing she'd ever heard. But I was watching her friend's face – the way she suddenly looked as though the cigarette was full of cow dung.

'The Black Adidas Gang,' I mused.

Becky laughed. 'The Tailors,' she corrected me.

'Right,' I nodded. 'Right. And are you a Tailor too?'

'As if!'

'But you're wearing Adidas. Blue, admittedly, but still Adidas.'

'*Azure*, actually. And I do it because it upsets them. Who says only members of their silly gang get to wear Adidas? *I* can wear whatever *I* want.'

I nodded firmly to let her know I completely agreed. Then: 'How do you become a member?' I asked. 'Beating up people and stealing their bags seems like fun to me.'

She laughed again. 'They choose you. You don't choose them.' She pulled a face. 'It's all pathetically macho like that.'

'Hmmm,' I said, picking little nips out of the cigarette, thinking. Within seconds I'd destroyed it completely.

Becky hadn't asked me if I'd told a teacher about my bag, or asked me why I'd missed English. Or even the real reason for Mr Coleburn's Tannoy announcement. Which made me think she didn't need to know the answers. She was particularly dismissive of this gang –

this gang of which Drew was a member, if you believed her – and that made me wonder if she knew more about it than she was saying.

And the trainers too. When I'd been wandering the school looking out for them I hadn't seen a single pair of Adidas unless they'd been attached to a gang member – a Tailor. It wasn't just the black ones I hadn't seen, but any colour. Adidas were a popular brand everywhere but Brook High School. Which meant the company ought to get their marketing team here pretty bloody sharpish. All those wasted adverts!

Becky was still watching me, seemingly still amused by me. 'My friend wants to go,' she said. 'Her toothache's really bad, you know.'

'I'd hate you to miss your appointment,' I told the friend, who sneered at me.

Becky was turning to leave. 'Make sure you say hello to me in English tomorrow.'

'I might not be there,' I said. She tutted at me in mock disgust. 'But what about tonight?'

She giggled. 'Are you asking me out?'

'I'm new, remember. I want to make friends. Why don't you take me where everybody goes around here?'

'Why don't I indeed?' she wondered.

I smiled up at her. 'Becky what?' I asked.

'Becky Chase.'

'So where should we meet tonight, Becky Chase?'

She faced me again, hands on hips, shining eyes narrowed. She was stunning, beautiful. After a long pause for thought she asked, 'Do you know The Angles snooker club?'

'I can find it.'

'It's on Eccles Lane, behind the cinema. How does half past seven sound?'

'Like a date.'

'A date it is, then, John Malarkey.'

'A date it is.'

She linked arms with her friend and walked away in the opposite direction to Brook. I watched her go. Her azure trainers looked very bright against the pavement.

SEVEN

The afternoon slouched by. I missed my Walkman, which was in my bag, which was in Mr Coleburn's office. I'm one of those people who never goes anywhere without having their ears plugged in, preferring more often than not to listen to music rather than my own thoughts. There was a lot of cloud: the brave sun from earlier had long disappeared but at least it didn't rain. The feeling that I was now up against the clock, with wasted hours slipping by before the Head of Year would make his threat real, didn't help. But I had to wait, because I couldn't do anything until the end of the day – except keep an impatient and frustrated eye on my watch.

I was on Raymond Avenue at exactly 3.30 when the school kicked out. There were kids everywhere, flooding the pavements and the road, boisterous and noisy, as if the end of the school day was an unexpected delight and they were determined to enjoy it to the full. They climbed into parents' waiting cars or went flying past on bikes or simply hurried by in huddles thick with another day's gossip. I stayed one step away. Not being a part of the crowd was nothing new for me; even at my old school I'd always been a distance-keeper – albeit not always a happy one. It was just my nature.

I hung around hoping I looked like I was waiting for a friend – which is what I *was* doing, kind of. Not that I was holding out much hope of being able to spot Simon Penn of 11B. Brook also had gates on Underhill Way and

Straub Street but I'd decided on Raymond Ave because it was out of sight of both the staff room and the teachers' car park. Knowing the way my luck was running today, however, Simon probably used both of those gates regularly and had never set foot through this entrance in his life.

I was also on the lookout for Tailors. And I did spot the Grunter, and was in two minds whether or not to follow him, if only to ask him what on earth my number meant. I'd been trying to figure it out for most of the afternoon and still hadn't come up with an answer (although I doubted it was a raffle ticket). I let him go, watching him turn in the direction of the shops again, deciding it was more important to talk to Simon. But when the flood of kids became a trickle, and then began to dry up altogether, I was disappointed if not surprised that he hadn't appeared.

Which left Plan B.

I hovered at the gates, with the grey monstrosity of the main block filling a much too large chunk of my vision. I couldn't help but feel reluctant to set foot on school grounds again, remembering the feelings of paranoia and claustrophobia it had been such a relief to leave behind. Neither did I want to run into Mr Coleburn or Mr Macallan, because I was certain that if they got their hands on me now they'd never let go – they'd probably squabble over who got to keep my scalp after they'd finished with me. The problem was, I simply didn't have any other option.

I was quick to make my way round the back of the empty school towards the gym block, keeping my head down as I hurried across the tennis courts. Out on the field there was a raucous, muddy football match under way, which I took as a practice for the game tomorrow afternoon. At least it meant the gym block was in use: I wouldn't look so conspicuous hanging around if there were a few players running back and forth from the changing rooms. So walking normally, looking as particularly unfurtive as I could, I marched through the doors where I'd seen Blondie and Spike disappear with my bag what seemed like days rather than hours before.

School gyms are the same the world over, I'm sure. You either love them or hate them. Personally, I'm not your stereotypical sports fan and I've locked horns with several PE teachers. Not only that, but teenagers and PE leave a distinctive odour; it's a mix of rubber soles, sour sweat and cheap anti-perspirant. No school gym is immune, especially not Brook.

Echoing voices and the hollow thump of bouncing balls carried around the whole block; a whistle blew shrilly, twice. I guessed there was some after-school club or other on the go. I crept along, not wanting the soles of my own trainers to squeak on the tiled floor. The door to the teachers' office was closed, more than likely locked. There were notice boards on either side of the corridor promoting exercise and healthy eating, dates for school sport fixtures, as well as the ubiquitous No Smoking posters with famous athletes looking serious. (It was this kind of condescension that had started me smoking in the first place.)

I wasn't sure what I was looking for exactly; I'd just got it in my head that this could be the gang's secret meeting place. The problem was, where could a group of kids hide from the teachers in the smallest block in the school? Although I'd read a book once where a sadistic secret society had met in the storeroom next to the gym. I wondered if the Tailors had read the same one.

The main corridor had a couple of branches off it: one way led to the gym itself, another to the changing rooms and a smaller sports hall. The gym was in use – basketball – hence the voices and whistle. The teacher putting the kids through their paces was Mr Scapa; an arrogant, bullying man who got a kick out of picking on the fat kids, the gangly kids, the slow kids – anyone not naturally inclined to sport.

I was careful he didn't see me, waiting for him to have moved out of sight to give some girl grief about the way she held the ball, then quickly tried the door of the store cupboard. Inside it was a jumble of five-a-side nets, badminton equipment, volleyballs and the like. You could perhaps swing a cat – as long as you didn't mind giving it a terrible headache. But there wasn't enough room for the furtive meetings of some nefarious secret society – fictional or otherwise. And I guessed I should have known better – none of the Tailors I'd seen so far had looked much like readers.

I closed the door quietly and made my way along the corridor's other branch to the sports hall. There was climbing apparatus and ropes hanging from the ceiling, a vaulting horse and balancing beams. Its small storeroom was full of crash mats. Which only left the two changing rooms, and I doubted very much they'd make a particularly private setting for planning the theft of report cards. My theory about a meeting place was fading fast.

I decided to check out the boys' changing room all

the same, not thinking I was going to find anything interesting, but not wanting to admit I'd hit another dead end just yet. I knew I'd been in there myself – twice in fact, for my own games lessons – but maybe there was another store cupboard or something I'd not noticed.

I double-checked I was alone before sticking my head in through the door. I didn't want to go inside because the last thing I needed was to get caught prowling and perhaps have yet another accusation of stealing flung at me. I immediately saw what I already knew anyway: it was a rectangular room with scratched and dented grey lockers all around the walls, several aisles of wooden benches in the middle, but nowhere to hide and whisper. The toilets and showers were just beyond, but I wasn't going to bother looking in there. The smell of feet was stronger; the room was gloomy and airless. Some lads hadn't bothered to use the lockers and their clothes were strewn across the benches, shoes and trainers shoved underneath.

I pulled my head out.

But stuck it right back inside again. There was a pair of black Adidas placed neatly on top of a bench next to somebody's clothes. They were displayed as a warning, or a boast. I stared at them. I was wondering what size they were, and if they'd fit me.

I might get to hear a few secrets if people believed I was a Tailor. I might be able to ask a few more questions. That's what I was thinking. And they'd make great footwear for tonight's date with Becky Chase.

So I crept inside.

They were a size eight; I was a nine, but reckoned I could

squeeze into them. Only one stripe of the logo had been blacked out – I was building a theory on what these stripes might mean, but didn't have time to think it through right now.

The trainers smelled foul, probably because whoever's they were never dreamed of leaving home without them. I spotted a can of Lynx poking out from underneath a pile of clothes and I gave them a quick spray. It didn't help much, just sweetened the stink, like rotting jelly babies. I couldn't walk out with them in my hand, point-blank refused to stick them up my jumper, and was searching around for a plastic bag or something to hide them in when I heard the rattle of football boots on smooth tiles coming along the corridor.

Immediately I put the trainers back on the bench exactly as they'd been, but panic made me clumsy and I dropped the can of deodorant. It sounded louder than smashing glass as it clattered on the changing-room floor, skittering away from me. I had to fumble under the bench for it. Come on, come on – swearing under my breath. I was hoping the football boots would stop or carry on straight past. But my luck, being *my* luck, meant they just got closer. I managed to grab the can of deodorant and shoved it back under the pile of clothes, trying not to ruffle them. Then I was quick to dive through into the shower room.

I hid in a toilet cubicle – the door pushed to but not locked, crouched on the seat so my feet wouldn't be seen underneath. Two voices came into the changing room.

'You're faking,' one said.

'It's killing me,' the second replied. 'Look, it's swelling up already.'

'Bollocks.'

'I landed funny when I dived for the penalty. I must have bent it back the wrong way or something.'

'I thought goalies were taught how to dive without hurting themselves.'

I didn't have to strain to listen: they thought they were alone and their voices boomed in the close changing room.

The second voice said, 'Why don't you get Harper to do it? He might have to sub me anyway if my wrist swells up any worse.'

'We haven't got Harper's mobile,' the first voice told him. 'We've got yours.'

There was a considered pause before the second voice asked, 'Have you got it on you now?'

The first voice chuckled quietly. 'If I say yes, are you going to fight me for it? Come on, Davie, have a go if you want. But careful of that poorly wrist.'

The second voice, Davie the goalie, was quiet.

I fidgeted awkwardly, silently; my legs were going to sleep underneath me as I crouched. I wanted to see faces and was tempted to risk pushing open the door a centimetre wider. I shuffled for a better position.

The first voice chuckled again. '*I've* not got it, Davie, but I've seen it. And it's got lots and lots of numbers in its memory. Your mum and dad, granny too. Can you imagine the kind of texts we're going to send them? Shocking language, dirty words.' The voice was clearly enjoying himself. 'You've got Sarah Short's number as well, haven't you? She's got great tits – I fancy her myself, you know. We could send her some juicy texts too. Not lies, just the kind of stuff you're too chicken to say to her face.' He laughed fully. 'No, no, better than that, let's send Jordan Cooper something juicy. I saw you eyeing him up in the showers the other day . . .'

I still couldn't see anything. I leaned forward and put my eye to the crack of the door.

There was an edge of aggression to Davie's voice. 'I know, okay? I've heard it all before. And not just from you.' He let it go, however; probably realized fists would be useless. He asked quietly, 'But what can I do if I'm injured? It's not my fault then, is it? Not if—'

'And everybody will know who's sent the messages, because technology's a wonderful thing, and your number will be displayed on their phones.'

Davie was quiet. There was a part of me that wondered what the fuss was about exactly. If somebody sends other kids dodgy messages on your phone, just explain to them what happened. But then again, I supposed, maybe it was nowhere near as easy as that. Because those other kids probably wouldn't care how true your explanations were, as long as they had a reason to humiliate you.

Public humiliation is most people's worst nightmare, and yet also fantastic sport. And because one kid is so scared of it, so scared of being shunned and shamed, they'll pick up on any little reason to shun and shame the next kid along – if *you* take the piss out of *him*, then *they* won't be picking on *you*. It's cruel.

Kids never forget either, not the important facts. We may let maths equations and historical dates slide out of our minds, but the cringe-inducing secrets of when X made a fool of themselves in front of Y on this day of the month at this time, will never be forgotten. And if you are X, you can absolutely guarantee it will be brought up over and over and over again for the rest of your life.

So, yes, I guessed I could understand Davie the goalie's predicament. And also acknowledge the sly intelligence of his blackmailer.

I shifted forward the tiniest amount, wanting to ease the door open that fraction more. The plastic toilet seat suddenly shifted and bowed underneath me. I froze again, holding my breath, trying to make my body as light as possible. I didn't dare make a single noise. The blackmailer, who I didn't doubt for a second was a Tailor, was bound to recognize me. But I needed to see faces.

'So it's up to you,' the blackmailer/Tailor told Davie. 'But it's the final—'

'Of course it is. That's why it's so important. You let in the goals tomorrow, make sure we lose the match, and you'll get your mobile back. How simple is that?'

Davie was quiet again.

'Simple as simple can be,' the blackmailer answered for him.

I waited for the goalie to respond, or for the blackmailer to walk away, but nothing happened. They must have been staring each other out. I could feel the tension. I got the impression that Davie was a big lad – goalies often are – and that he would have loved to take a swing, have a go.

Maybe I could see over the top of the door if I stood up? I slowly reached out my arms to push against the cubicle walls on either side of me, to steady myself – and bit by bit, little by little, I straightened up, tried to stand. The toilet seat bent underneath me again, but I didn't think dangerously so. I eased myself silently higher, keeping my head down until I could just about see.

I was about to poke my head over the top when a mobile phone rang.

I nearly slipped off the buckled seat in surprise, the shock locking my knees, but my feet slipping on the shiny plastic. I pushed hard against the cubicle walls. I was managing to keep myself from crashing face first onto the floor by what seemed like sheer willpower. And I was shouting in my head, Please God don't let it be my phone! *Please* not my phone!

It wasn't.

The Tailor said, 'Yeah?' He walked from the changing room into the shower area, stood right outside the cubicle I was hiding in. 'Yeah, I'm talking to him . . . No worries, he'll be fine . . . Yeah, yeah. He understands.' He was talking loud enough for Davie to hear.

I was teetering on the edge of the toilet seat, but could feel the thin plastic buckling and bending beneath me. Either it was going to slide out from under my feet, or simply snap from my weight. Both would dump me down the filthy pan. Whichever, I was in the shit – literally.

I was glad I'd had the foresight to leave the door slightly ajar. If it had been closed and locked it would have been obvious someone was in here. I doubted the Tailors tolerated spies. But then again, the more I felt the seat shift underneath me, the more I thought that at least if the door had been locked it would be harder for the blackmailer to get in at me.

I held my breath and pretended I was a feather.

The Tailor was saying, 'Just a little twinge in his wrist is all. Davie's a big lad, he can handle it.' But then he dropped his voice. 'Who? The new kid?'

My ears pricked up.

'So he's on the run from Coleburn, so what? What can he do . . . ? He can ask as many questions as he wants, he's still— Yeah, I know . . . Yeah, of course . . . But he's still screwed, isn't he? Coleburn's not even looking for anyone else . . . No worries, I'd love to have a go. I never liked the look of him anyway, strutting around like he's special or something . . . I'll do it tomorrow . . . No, no worries, I'll enjoy it. I guarantee he won't be going round asking any more questions. His fault for being the new kid, isn't it . . . ?'

I stayed absolutely, perfectly still. But I was burning up with wanting to ring some bastard's neck. His tone of voice told me I was just an insect that needed to be crushed. Everything I'd suspected was proved true by that one conversation. They'd needed someone to take the fall, so why not pick on the new kid? Who gave a toss about someone they didn't know?

The blackmailer's phone beeped as he cut the call. 'Let's get that wrist strapped up, eh, Davie?' he said as he walked back though to the changing room. 'Mr Scapa should have some bandages. He'll not want to see his star keeper out of action for tomorrow's big match, will he?' He led the goalie back out into the corridor.

My muscles had stiffened with the strain; I eased myself down off the seat and stepped out of the cubicle, flexing my shoulders and arms. I wanted to get out as fast as I could. Not because I was scared, but because I was angry. If I came face to face with a Tailor right now I might want to push my luck. I snatched up the black Adidas that were still on the bench as I hurried into the corridor.

I still didn't have anything to hide them in, so ended up reluctantly stuffing them inside my zipped-up jacket, one under each arm so the bulge didn't show.

There were voices coming from the teachers' office at the end of the corridor; the door was open. I scanned the notice boards, running a finger over the papers pinned there, looking for the football fixtures. I found what I was after: the game tomorrow against Stonner Secondary School. The Year Eleven inter-school final, which was why we'd all been given the afternoon off to watch it. I told myself I'd be there to cheer the home team on.

As I scooted by the office I saw the blackmailer with his back to me, but I recognized Big George all the same. If he'd turned round he would have seen me. He didn't, and I was too quick to the outside doors anyway.

Mr Scapa was saying, 'It's not even bruised, David. I doubt you've twisted it. You'll be fine for tomorrow.'

'That's lucky, eh, Davie?' Big George said.

But Davie didn't reply.

TROUBLE MAGNET

EIGHT

The builders had packed up for the day and gone by the time I got home. Not a bad job, I thought, being a builder – they were never there when I left for school, and very rarely still around when I got home again. I reckoned I could do with a job that left me with a lot of spare time. To be fair to them, I could see what they'd done today, however, because the sign was above the door.

Black on red, the letters painted to cast long shadows: 'JM BOOKS'.

Not particularly inspiring maybe. But Mum was Jess, I was John, we were both Malarkey, so we liked it. And perhaps this would be my job when I left school – I could work with Mum.

To be honest, I didn't have a clue what I wanted to do. Some people told me there was a whole world of possibility, others claimed that world was only possible if you sweated hard at school, jumped through the right hoops and passed all your exams. And then there were those who said it was a shit world anyway, millions unemployed, and nothing you did would make a difference or make you happy. Just what was a teenager supposed to believe? That's what I wanted to know.

So why should I be getting all hot and bothered about being kicked out and maybe missing doing my GCSEs? If I got myself excluded, my fault. If I messed up my life, my fault. If someone else tried to mess up my life for me? I wasn't going down without a fight.

There was a back entrance, but I let myself in at the front of the shop because I wanted to see what other progress had been made. Not much, was the answer. It had been a florist's when we'd bought it, before that a grocer's, and I still reckoned you could smell potatoes and daffodils and damp. The guts of the old shop had been ripped out but the posh new shelves Mum had ordered seemed a long way off from being put up just yet. I walked through to the back stairs with rubble crunching under my feet. We'd also bought the flat above. I wasn't sure which was the biggest bombsite.

'It's me,' I shouted as I ducked into my bedroom — the only room to at least look ordered, but I still had a couple of boxes at the end of my bed that needed unpacking. I changed quickly out of my grubby school uniform and hid my new trainers under the bed. I didn't want Mum asking questions.

I still didn't know if the school had been in touch with her and was a little nervous about seeing her. I didn't want her to know anything about what had happened today. Not because I thought she'd 'tell me off' — she wasn't that kind of parent; I'd never been 'spanked' or 'grounded'. She'd believe me, she wouldn't doubt my innocence for a second, but it would worry her, upset her — especially the thought of me getting kicked out and missing my exams. She had enough worries right now without me adding to them. I was determined to sort everything out for myself.

I found her in what would be the living room if we

brought the settee in from the landing and set up the TV and video. Before we could do that we'd have to shift the boxes of books. And before we could do that Mum would have to stop reading them.

'Hi. I'm home,' I said, only poking my head round the door, wary of her reaction to me if Mr Coleburn had called her.

She greeted me with a smile. 'Hi yourself. Good day?'

Her smile meant everything was okay and I stepped through into the room – but decided to ignore her question. 'Is this your system of quality control?' I asked.

She peered at me over the top of her glasses, over the top of the paperback book she was holding. 'Hmm?'

'Do you have to read them before you can sell them?'

She lowered the book with a sigh and pushed her glasses up onto the top of her head, where they were immediately lost in the flowing blonde curls. 'I don't want to miss out on a good one,' she said.

'Is that one a good one?'

She pondered the cover for a moment. 'Not bad, but those there are the ones I'm going to keep.' She gestured at several neat stacks pushed up against the wall.

'You're not going to sell them?'

'They're the kind of books I know I'll want to read again.' I made a show of looking at the boxes full of books, some yet to be opened, others that spilled out onto the floor. Mum was surrounded by them, cut off like a castaway on a desert island of visible carpet.

'But there're so many books,' I told her. 'How can you have time to re-read any?'

'Some books you should always re-read. The important ones.'

'And don't think I'm trying to be funny or anything,' I said, 'but shouldn't we really be selling them? Seeing as we're a bookshop.'

She pulled a face at my sarcasm. 'We'll sell plenty of books.'

'Just not the good ones.'

'No, no. We *have* to sell good books. I'm not going to sell crap, Johnny. I wouldn't be able to look at myself in the mirror if I did.'

I looked confused – on purpose. 'So you don't want to sell your favourite books, but you refuse to sell the ones you don't like either. So what are we going to sell? I've got a feeling I might starve before you decide.'

'Isn't it a sin to tease your doting mother?' she asked me reproachfully, with a single eyebrow raised.

'If it is,' I answered, 'then they've had my hotel room in Hell booked for years.'

She laughed. I liked it when I made her laugh. She hadn't been doing enough of it lately. Her knees popped as she stood up, making me wonder how long she'd been sitting there. 'I've been blessed with an evil child,' she told me. 'One who wants his tea, probably.'

I followed her through to the flat's cramped kitchen. It would have been kind of small even without the boxes on the worktop and breakfast bar; *with* them it was an obstacle course. We'd only unpacked the things we needed: two plates, two mugs, the kettle, the toaster – those kinds of things. We were still a long way from settling here, I realized. So far, it didn't feel like we particularly wanted to.

I watched her put the kettle on and ferret around in

the fridge for the quiche we hadn't finished yesterday. At least she wasn't still dressed in her pyjamas; she was bothering to put on jeans and T-shirt nowadays. I hadn't liked the way the builders looked at her when she'd wandered down to them with cups of tea in her pyjamas. She was thirty-five, looked younger, lots of unruly blonde hair. She was still slim and had never felt the need to wear make-up. 'Nice mum you've got there,' one girning plasterer had winked at me. 'Fuck off,' I'd told him.

'The sign's up,' I said. 'Looks good.'

Mum brightened again. 'Yes, it does, doesn't it? I'm glad they've put it up so soon. I've been down three times just to stand in the street and look at it. Did you know you can see it all the way from the building society on the corner?'

'Cool,' I said.

She nodded, smiling at me. 'Yes. It is. In fact, it's beautiful.'

We grinned at each other.

'Grandma and Grandad would be pleased,' I said tentatively.

She nodded again, but wouldn't look at me. 'Yes. I think they would.'

Mum had only been nineteen when she'd had me. She'd been a 'rum lass', as Grandma often put it, and my dad had never entered the picture. I'd never known him, doubted I ever would. He'd been called Robert and I had his eyes, but that was all I knew. We'd lived with Grandma and Grandad and whenever the subject of my father came up they'd always made sure I had plenty of love.

Their deaths hit us hard. A jack-knifing HGV on the

motorway had crushed the life out of them in a split-second, in an instant. They'd never stood a chance. But the money they'd left behind had bought this flat and the shop below; it had bought my mother's biggest ambition. I knew she had a hard time rectifying the two things in her head. It confused me some nights too, as I lay awake in bed. How can so much loss and pain buy your dreams?

I guessed it was why Mum had wanted to move so far away. Not because she was callous; simply for a new start – just us now, not so many reminders and memories.

So this was our new start, our new life. And part of it was me giving up smoking; I'd promised Mum I already had. I hated going behind her back, keeping secrets from her. We often talked about the fact that we only had each other nowadays, and about how we had to look out for each other, keep each other close. How close could two people be when one of them kept secrets?

'We've not got much salad left,' she told me. 'Plenty of hummus, luckily.'

'Yeah, lucky,' I said half under my breath, and was very pleased I'd had the fish and chips earlier.

We ate off our laps in the living room, sitting side by side on chairs meant for the kitchen, big mugs of tea by our feet. On a closed box in front of us was Mum's sketched drawing of how she'd like the inside of the shop to look.

'Should I use the Dewey Decimal System?' Mum asked. 'But I'm not sure which number stands for which subject.'

'That's libraries, isn't it? Not bookshops.'

'I'd like to stock a little non-fiction as well,' she said. 'Maybe just these shelves here.'

'What kind of non-fiction?'

'Biographies mainly – I think they sell quite well. But some of those self-help books too, because they seem to be popular . . .' She saw the look on my face. 'Don't be like that,' she chided. 'Some of them are very interesting.'

I snorted through my nose at her. I'd never been a fan of those kinds of books.

She tutted and shook her head at me. 'How did you turn out so cynical so young?' she wondered.

'Grandad,' I told her.

'Hmmm,' she agreed. 'I can see the old codger in you.'

It was true enough. Grandad had an opinion on absolutely everything, and he'd always been willing to share. I'd spent many hours on long walks or late at night having them drummed into me. I missed him; his sharp blue eyes, his whisky-breath, his strong hand ruffling my hair, and the way he laughed when I gave an opinion at the dinner table which turned out to be something he'd told me the night before repeated almost verbatim. He'd been a heavy smoker when I was younger, but had packed it in several years ago. I remembered him stubbing his last one out in the ashtray I'd bought him for his fiftieth birthday. 'That's it,' he'd growled. 'No more. It's a mug's game.' And I never did see him with another one. He had that kind of willpower – something I wasn't lucky enough to inherit, obviously.

I wondered what he'd say about my problems at school. 'Meet the bastards head on, Johnny.' That's what his advice would be. 'If you're in the right, never back down.'

Mum and I finished our meal in silence, both a little lost in our mutual sadness.

I took our plates into the kitchen. Mum had left most

of her meal. I shouted through, 'Do you mind if I go out tonight?'

'Don't be silly. Of course I don't.'

I scraped her plate into the Tesco carrier bag we were using as a bin. 'There's this snooker hall where some of the kids from school go, apparently. I just wanted to see what it was like.'

'Sounds good,' she called. 'Are you meeting anyone there?'

I thought about Becky Chase. 'Not really,' I lied. 'But there should be a few faces I'll know.' I thought about Blondie, Spike et al.

'Don't walk home if it's late,' she told me. 'Get a taxi, okay?'

'Okay,' I said.

I was thinking about what I'd overheard Spike saying in the changing rooms today, about making sure I wouldn't ask any more questions. I realized that if any Tailors were there tonight, and they wanted to stop me asking questions, it might not be a taxi I needed to get me home. It might be an ambulance.

NINE

'You're late, John Malarkey,' Becky Chase accused me.

I shrugged my apology, ran a hand through my wet hair. 'It's pouring down,' I told her.

There were a couple of older lads collecting cues and balls and chalk, but Becky was alone. 'I'll let you off if you buy me a drink,' she decided.

I watched the older lads pay a deposit and head through to the tables. Neither of them was wearing Adidas.

I was late getting to the snooker club because Eccles Lane was little more than an alleyway that cut across the High Street and I'd walked past the opening twice without realizing. It wasn't until I remembered Becky saying it was behind the cinema that I managed to find it. I had a natural aversion to dark alleys, and especially disliked being led up them by people I didn't trust. Not that I was going to turn back, however, not after walking this far in too tight trainers that hurt my feet.

Once I was inside, The Angles was nothing like the smoke-fugged dive I'd been expecting. It was bright, plush and modern. The front foyer was carpeted, with posters advertising only the most up-to-date designer drinks hanging on the wall. There were a couple of flashing quiz machines, but someone had had the sense to turn the sound down on the annoying electronic music and chimes they usually blared. The counter where you paid for your game and could buy soft drinks and snacks was at the far end; the guy working behind it wore a waistcoat with a discreet triangle of red balls embroidered over his breast pocket. He'd been chatting to Becky when I walked in, and he now served us a glass of Coke each. A door to the left of the counter led to the over-eighteens bar while the snooker tables were through to the right.

'Have you been waiting long?' I asked.

'I've only been sitting here for about five minutes,' she said. 'But I've been looking forward to seeing you again *all* afternoon.'

I chuckled. 'And why should I believe you?'

'Because I have sincere eyes,' she told me.

She'd asked for a straw with her Coke and she used it to stir the ice cubes, making them rattle against the sides of the glass. I found it difficult not to stare at her. Out of school uniform she looked eighteen, easily. She leaned against the wall, seeming to concentrate more on her drink than me.

I was here because I thought she knew about the Tailors, I told myself, but admitted it was because I fancied her as well. Which I reckoned was a scary admission.

She was wearing her blue trainers and I was curious to know what she'd say when she noticed the black pair I was sporting. I'd nearly chickened out of putting them on earlier, deciding it was a foolish/dangerous thing to do. But I'd told myself I needed answers quick, I needed to meet certain kinds of people, and walking around in black Adidas was a sure route to provoking a reaction one way or another.

'So, are you going to tell me, then?'

I wasn't sure what she meant. 'Tell you what?'

'Why you wanted to meet me tonight.'

'I thought it was obvious,' I said. 'We were getting on so well at the bus stop this afternoon, I thought it'd be wrong not to meet again.' I noticed the lad behind the counter was doing a bad job of cleaning some glasses, and a worse job of pretending not to listen. I wasn't going to talk with him hovering. I saw the jukebox on the wall and steered Becky towards it.

'It's mostly rubbish,' she informed me as I flipped through the tracks.

'I don't know . . . The Beatles, the Rolling Stones . . .' I had a pound coin ready to push into the slot.

Becky snorted at me. 'Just how old *are* you, John Malarkey?'

I felt my neck redden, the colour rise all the way up to my cheeks. 'It's the kind of stuff my grandad always played,' I said. Then realized exactly what it was I'd said, and blushed even harder. My face would have been hot to the touch. Was it any wonder I didn't feel as though I fitted in with kids my own age? 'Maybe there's something a bit more charty,' I said lamely, continuing to flip, but holding onto my pound.

Becky was staring at me like I was an animal she'd only ever seen in pictures before, never in real life. And I felt like a creature at the zoo. There was a slight smile on her lips – which could have been laughing at me; I wasn't sure.

We were out of earshot of the lad behind the counter now. 'I'm in a lot of trouble,' I told her. 'The Tailors set me up. I could get kicked out of Brook, but I'm guessing you already know that . . .'

She raised her eyebrows at me, but said nothing, sipped her drink instead.

'Who's the boss of the Tailors, Becky?' I asked. I pointed at her trainers. 'Is it you?'

She laughed out loud, literally squealed with pleasure at the thought of it. The lad behind the counter looked up suddenly, and I locked eyes with him until he turned away again.

'You're so *funny*,' she said. 'You should be on TV!'

I didn't reply, just took note of the fact that she hadn't exactly denied my accusation. Which might seem like a bizarre conclusion to jump to, but it stemmed from the theory I'd been building about black Adidas.

This was my thinking: Dominic Dom was the wettest behind the ears, he'd been performing the most dangerous task, and he'd had all three stripes of his Adidas on display (but maybe now he'd been allowed to black one out). Blondie, Spike and Slim had done the tricky stuff – stealing my bag, selling the report cards – and they'd had a single stripe blacked out. Big George obviously had been giving the orders to Slim at lunch time, was pulling Davie the goalie's strings too, and had blackened two of his stripes. I'd got the idea that it was a ranking system, a hierarchy. The more important you were in the Tailors' scheme of things, the more stripes you filled in black.

Becky Chase was wearing a different colour altogether; a more obvious colour too, the only blue pair I'd seen. It made me wonder how high up the hierarchy she was.

I waited for her to look at me again, then held her gaze. I was willing to push her, to find out exactly how right I was, but a face I recognized caught my eye.

Simon Penn hurried through from the area with the snooker tables. He was still wearing his school uniform.

He had his head down and looked to me like he was desperately trying to hold back tears. I reached out to grab him.

'Simon. Hey, you okay?'

He didn't recognize me at first and twisted himself out of my grip. Then when it clicked who I was he said, 'I don't know what to do. I've told him I can't do everything in time and—' Then he spotted Becky Chase. He shut up immediately, shook his head. He tried to get away.

I grabbed his arm and pulled him to one side. 'What's going on?'

His eyes flicked down to my feet, and his whole expression changed when he saw the trainers I was wearing. He suddenly got angry, his damp eyes hardening. Now I didn't have a hope in hell of talking to him. He stormed out into the rainy darkness of Eccles Lane.

I wanted to chase him but he was running.

I turned back to Becky, who was smiling at me, sipping her drink. 'What peculiar friends you have, John Malarkey.'

I stared hard at her. She didn't flinch. I saw the lad behind the counter watching us and made sure my look told him to mind his own business.

Becky flicked her hair over her shoulder, as if signalling a change of subject. 'I'm still waiting for you to ask me.'

I didn't know what she meant. 'Ask you what?' I said a little too sharply.

She tutted at my tone. But with another sip of her drink said, 'If Jade's teeth are any better.'

I cottoned on quickly; with a sigh and a sip of my own drink I decided to play along. 'Right, your friend from the bus stop. She's not here tonight?' Becky shook her head. 'But the dentist was nice to her, was he? He didn't have to pull anything out and cause her any excessively horrible and sickening pain, did he?'

'We didn't really need to go,' Becky said. And as if to prove it she crunched an ice cube between her teeth. 'It was just an excuse.'

'But the teachers believed you because of your sincere eyes.'

She laughed at this. 'Hey, you learn quick, John Malarkey.'

I asked, 'So where did you go?' Because I guessed I was meant to.

'To meet Jade's boyfriend. He's at another school.'

'That's nice,' I said slowly, not sure where this was heading.

'Would you like to meet mine?'

'Your boyfriend?' I hoped I managed to kill the treacherous twitch of disappointment in my voice.

She nodded. 'I've told him all about you,' she said.

'Okay,' I said hesitantly. 'Is he here?'

'He's playing pool. He'll like your trainers.'

She turned and walked through to the snooker tables, didn't even turn to check and see if I was following. It was obvious I would be.

But I walked over to the counter first, and liked the way the lad backed away a step as I approached. I leaned over to look at his feet; he was wearing shiny shoes. 'Just checking,' I told him with a smile.

There were eight full-size tables, only half of them being played tonight – with the *crack* or *snick* of the balls, and the *thunk* of a pot, audible over the subdued jukebox music. Beyond and down a single step was a smaller L-shaped area with seating around the walls, covered green to match the baize. There were a dozen pool and billiard tables, two of these in use, and nobody wearing Adidas so far. A TV screen high up in one corner showed a continuous loop of trailers from movies old and new. A lad whose face I wasn't sure if I recognized or not was playing by himself at a table around the bend of the L.

'This is Freddie,' Becky told me. 'Freddie Cloth. He's in our English class too. Freddie, I'd like you to meet that boy I was talking about, John Malarkey.'

He took his shot, potting the black, finishing up, and only then acknowledged my presence with a nod. He was dark-haired, shorter than me, skinnier than me, but there was an edge of sharpness about him – like broken glass. When he stepped out from behind the table I could see the Adidas he was wearing. All three white stripes had been blackened. He slid his cue across the tabletop: game over.

'Malarkey?' he mused. 'Isn't that just another word for bullshit?'

TEN

In a parallel universe I would have been having fun with friends, maybe at the cinema, maybe at a concert, maybe even on a picture-postcard beach in the Caribbean. In this universe, however, I was standing watching Becky Chase and Freddie Cloth sucking face while having my toes tingle painfully in too tight trainers. And I instantly knew Becky wasn't in charge of the Tailors. This guy was the boss.

'It's very clever,' I lied. 'Your name's Cloth, and you call your gang the Tailors. I'm very impressed.'

He thinned his lips at my sarcasm, but you couldn't have called it a smile. His eyes didn't reflect much, seemed very hard, more like smooth stone. He wore expensive clothes, all labels proudly displayed, but they didn't suit him quite like they did his girlfriend. 'You any good?' He gestured at the pool table.

'Not bad.'

'Fancy a game?'

'If you're paying.'

He crouched down by the side of the table and fed it some money. The balls rumbled noisily to the opening at the far end. Becky seemed to be having the time of her life. She handed me a cue, her face flushed with excitement. Her boyfriend set up the balls, placing them in the correct pattern in the triangle. Then he flipped a coin. 'Heads or tails?'

'Heads.'

'Tails,' he said. 'My break.' But he must have forgotten to show me the coin.

He bent low over the table, took his shot, and the balls opened with a *crack*. He stepped aside to let me get at the table, and as I walked round to the cue ball I noticed somebody else had joined us: Blondie stood to one side. Freddie Cloth hadn't planned on facing me alone.

'Hey, Ev.' He nodded. 'Glad you could make it.'

'Bodyguard?' I asked.

'Take your best shot,' Freddie Cloth told me. He may even have meant at pool.

My hands were shaking as I leaned over the table, because I began to realize the mistake I'd made by coming here tonight.

I told myself I was being ridiculous – what were they going to do in a public place? I tried to stay cool, tried not to make the shaking too obvious, but still missed potting the red I was aiming for. It would seem things weren't going my way.

Freddie was quick to get back to the table.

I moved to stand as far away from Blondie – Ev – as I could get. The problem was, keeping out of his reach was also keeping me round the bend in the room and out of sight of the other players. 'Hey, thanks for giving me my bag back,' I said, going for as much bravado as possible to hide the nerves. He didn't answer; he just glared at the stolen Adidas I was wearing.

'You don't deserve to wear those stripes,' Freddie told me as if he was a voice box for Blondie's brain. He potted a yellow. He walked around the table for his next shot, locking eyes with me for a brief second. 'It's an insult to all of us that you are.'

'I just felt a bit left out,' I said. 'I want to join. I want to be a Tailor too.'

'That's what Becky told me,' he said, potting a second ball. 'She said you've been asking lots of questions.' He missed his third.

My turn. 'You seem to have a lot of stuff on the go. Lots of money-making schemes. I could do with some money.' I missed again, rapped the table with my knuckles in disappointment. 'Hey, Cloth,' I said. 'You're wiping the floor with me.'

Becky giggled, until her boyfriend shot her a warning glance. She rolled her eyes as she sucked on her straw.

Freddie turned back to me. 'You're forgetting one thing,' he said. 'The Tailors run Brook; every one of us goes to school there.' He sank another ball. 'But you're about to get kicked out.'

I was keeping one eye on him and one eye on Blondie. Becky Chase sat quietly playing with the last slivers of ice in her glass; she could have been at the theatre. 'I see your point,' I said. 'Which is another reason I wanted to meet you. I don't want to get kicked out.'

'Tough,' Blondie growled.

'My God, it speaks,' I said, feigning surprise. 'You train them well,' I told Freddie. But nobody laughed.

Cloth stepped away again and I bent for my shot. 'I could be of use to you at football matches. I'm a real crap goalie already, so I wouldn't need to be black-mailed.' From the corner of my eye I caught the look that passed between Cloth and Blondie. They hadn't expected me to know about what was happening with tomorrow's match. I let myself smile, and at last managed to pot a ball. 'Unless you want me to think you up some messages you can text to Davie's parents?' Again, I hit the mark.

'You're really beginning to piss me off,' Freddie said nastily.

'Tough,' I replied, and winked at Becky, who grinned back. I was on a roll; potted another ball. Cloth was pissing me off too. Who the hell did he think he was with his juvenile gangster angst?

He narrowed his eyes at me. 'You're getting frustrating, Malarkey.'

'Frustrating like watching the National Society of Stutterers and Speech Impediments playing Snap?' I asked. 'Or frustrating like standing behind a fat kid in the lunch queue when there's only two puddings left?'

Becky Chase burst into laughter. She didn't even stop when her boyfriend scowled at her. 'Oh, come on, Freddie. You've got to admit, that was *funny*!'

I settled over the cue for my next shot, stupidly believing I was gaining control of the situation. 'You see, Freddie, I'm good at thinking up funny messages. We could text the whole world. I just—' But the words failed as Big George and one of the kids from the tuck shop (the one who'd called out my name) appeared from round the corner. I also fluffed my shot.

'Is he a comedian?' Big George asked.

'He likes to think he is,' Freddie replied through gritted teeth. I didn't like the way he held his cue as he stepped up to take his next shot. 'This is George and Hutty,' he introduced me. 'Looks like all my good friends have come to meet you.'

'You can tell they're the bad guys just by the shoes they wear,' I said.

The odds were quickly, scarily stacking up against me. Freddie Cloth's big talk maybe didn't worry me so much, but the way his cronies were gathering around him was not a good thing to be happening right now. I tried to stop my thoughts from showing on my face, but wasn't sure how well I was managing.

'Can you blame me for trying to find out what's going on?' I asked, ignoring the others as best I could and just focusing on Cloth. 'Do you expect me to just lie down and take it?'

'Do you expect me to confess to Coleburn and beg his forgiveness?' Freddie countered. 'Easier for everyone if you accept that you can't do anything about it,' he said seriously. 'So, yeah, that's exactly what we expect you to do.'

'Why me?' I asked.

'Why you?' he pondered. He flicked his gaze to Blondie and gave a quick nod. Blondie disappeared round the corner. Then back to me: 'Because we needed somebody to take the blame, somebody Coleburn could use as a scapegoat. Because you're not one of us, so what did we care?'

'"Not one of us" as in a *Tailor*?'

'You're not one of Brook,' Hutty from the tuck shop piped up.

'He's right,' Cloth told me, nodding at Hutty's supposed wisdom. 'I don't know where you come from, and I don't really give a toss either, but you're not Brook – so we chose you.'

I'd backed myself up against the wall, as far out of

reach as possible. It had been an unconscious action, and I now felt trapped. Especially seeing as I could hear Blondie telling the other pool players round the corner to make themselves scarce. My face must have been a picture when he returned with Spike in tow. They took up position next to Big George and Hutty from the tuck shop; my only exit barred.

All I could do was keep talking. 'So I'm an outsider, right? And you just want to look after your own – is that what you're telling me? Because that's a load of crap, Freddie. It's the rest of the Brook kids you're ripping off, isn't it?'

He played his shot. 'We provide *services* for them.'

'Services – right. Yeah, I didn't think you were real *gangsters*,' I said.

Big George was ready to lunge for me, but Freddie held him back with a look.

'It's all bullshit and bravado,' Cloth assured him.

The way he could read me, the way he could see right through me, was worrying. I pushed on anyway. 'Come on, Freddie, admit it. You're not clever enough to organize this by yourself. You can't keep it all underground, surely. Which teachers have you got involved?'

He laughed then. They all laughed. It must have been the funniest thing they'd heard all week; it was like thigh-slapping at a bad pantomime.

'I told you, Malarkey,' Cloth said. '*We* run Brook High: the Tailors. Teachers these days, they're far too busy to know what's really going on outside their sacred classrooms, especially in a school as big as ours.' He was potting balls all the time he was talking. 'Some are like Coleburn or Scapa, too bored or narrow-minded to give a shit. While most of the others, the ones who'd give a damn if they could, they're so busy worrying about league tables and privatization and how messed up the exam system is they don't get the chance to even notice us.' He looked up at me now, meeting my eye. 'We're clever – cleverer than you think. We keep it kind of low-key, kind of small; don't poke our heads above ground if we don't have to. We don't beat people up, or questions would be asked. We don't steal money, we *make* it – less questions asked.' He looked back at his game. 'Why do you think we only took Macallan's video card and driver's licence?'

I'd thought about this myself and knew the answer. 'The driver's licence is easily replaced, but just serious enough to get him all riled up. The video card has probably got you several DVDs out on rental already that you can sell.'

'An added bonus,' Cloth admitted.

'Nice touch with the family photo, by the way,' I said.

'That was my idea,' Becky suddenly chirped.

'Hey! Well done you!' I beamed at her.

She fluttered her eyelashes, pretended she was flattered.

Freddie wasn't at all impressed, so I said to him, 'It was a big risk, though, wasn't it? How did you know Macallan would let me wait in the office? Or that I'd even bother to let your thief in?'

'The risks are what get you the adrenaline rush,' he told me, and almost lazily potted the black. He shrugged. 'You lose,' he said.

I didn't see a signal; don't even know if he gave one. Suddenly the four Tailors were on me in the corner. I tried to swing my cue, but Hutty snatched it away, only to jab it back into my stomach. Big George and Blondie slammed me up against the wall, kicked my feet out from underneath me, and then the four of them bustled me to the floor behind the pool table. I had my face pushed into the carpet, the trainers torn off my feet. I fought back, struggled and kicked, and received a bust lip from Spike for my efforts. Freddie watched his underlings from a safe distance. They rolled me onto my back and pinned me down. And I thought to myself that I'd done a lot of running away today, so maybe it was about time I got caught.

Everybody laughed as Hutty used the cue chalk on my nose, rubbing it roughly, leaving a blue stain. Maybe later I'd feel pleased that it took four of them to keep me down, I was thinking. But the way Freddie stood over me holding the hard, solid, heavy white ball worried me. He squinted as if taking aim at the chalk mark on the tip of my nose. Then without warning he dropped the ball. The noise of it smacking me between the eyes sounded much louder inside my head.

I was seeing stars. I'd never known if you could before, thought it was a myth, but there they were, reds and greens, dancing in front of me. I tried to focus. 'Shit! That hurts! I thought you didn't beat people up?'

'Nobody's ever pissed us off as much as you, Malarkey. So you're our first.' Cloth met my fuzzy eyes with his cold, hard stare. 'So feel privileged, yeah?'

Big George laughed loudly at this; the rest of the Tailors grinned as well.

'See? I can do funny too,' Cloth told me, picking one of the balls I hadn't potted off the table, juggling it above me, taunting me. 'I wouldn't keep moving your head,' he said. 'You don't want to get this in your eye.'

He didn't just drop it this time; there was a flick of the wrist to give it some power. And it hit the left side of my face, exploding a whole bomb of pain on my cheekbone.

I gritted my teeth against it. 'Okay, okay! Jesus Christ! I get the picture. I take the hint, okay?'

Freddie took another couple of balls off the table and I was really wishing I'd managed to pot a few more. He gave one to Blondie, a second to Big George. 'This is a warning. You don't try and ask questions about us, or steal our stuff, or grass us up.'

Big George rubbed the ball between his hands as though he were polishing it up to be able to see his face in its smooth, hard shine. He was smiling at me. He was going to enjoy this.

'Everything okay?'

I felt the relief wash over me: maybe this time my luck was actually holding. It was the lad from behind the counter in his snazzy waistcoat. And I wasn't going to be shy about asking for a bit of a helping hand here.

'Hey! Quick!' I yelled. 'Quick! Get the manager!'

Everybody laughed again. They were definitely having more fun than me.

Freddie offered him a wide, welcoming smile. 'Hi there, Trev,' he said breezily. 'I told you we'd get your trainers back.'

I was hauled to my feet, pushed up against the wall. Blondie pinned me by the throat.

Freddie handed Trev a pool cue. 'Go on, Trev. It's your honour to teach him a lesson for stealing your trainers.' There were shouts of encouragement from the other

Tailors, and I thought my time was really up here. Trev stepped towards me, holding the cue like a baseball bat, getting ready to swing. I didn't think I was going to leave The Angles in one piece.

But Becky said, 'Why don't you let him join? If he wants to be in your gang, why not let him?'

I heard her. I wasn't sure if anybody else had, so I started agreeing loudly. 'That's all I want. I just want to be a Tailor.'

'Just smack him,' Big George told Trev.

'I'll do it,' Blondie offered.

I was talking quickly. 'That's why I stole the trainers, so I could be a Tailor. I like it that other kids are scared of you when you wear them—'

Blondie still had me by the throat and squeezed hard to shut me up.

Freddie, however, was listening. 'Just a minute,' he said, holding Trev back from taking that swing. 'Maybe that's not too bad an idea.' He ignored the disappointed murmurings from his gang, but I was grinning and nodding like mad – agreeing whole-heartedly. He put his arm round his girlfriend's shoulder. 'In fact I think it's the best idea I've heard all night.' He kissed Becky hard. She bent her leg behind her like all the best actresses in black and white movies used to do.

Blondie squeezed my throat again, digging his fingers in. I spluttered and coughed. He obviously didn't like the idea.

'No, leave him, Ev,' Freddie said. 'Let's give him a chance.'

'He's not Brook,' Spike said.

'True,' Freddie admitted. 'But that's why he's got to

prove himself, yeah? You've got to admit, he's got balls. It takes balls to walk in here to talk to me wearing a pair of black Adidas. What do you think, George?'

Big George seemed to be able to read something in Freddie's eyes that I couldn't. His doughy face creased into a thin smile. 'We'll let him tag along tonight. Let him prove himself.'

Blondie was still squeezing. 'I don't trust him.'

Freddie shrugged. 'Don't worry about it. He probably doesn't trust us either.' He came right up to my face and took hold of my chin. 'You don't trust us either, do you, Malarkey?' And because Blondie had my throat tight enough to constrict my words, Freddie shook my chin painfully, forcing me to shake my head. 'See?'

'And if he acts the arsehole?' Hutty asked.

The tip of Freddie's nose was a hair's breadth away from touching mine. 'Oh, I don't think he'd dare.'

ELEVEN

The house was in a quiet street, semi-detached, a small but neat front garden, just like the rest of the neighbours. Lights were on behind drawn curtains in all the windows; a gaggle of loud voices and the muffled thump of music could be heard here on the road. There was no car in the driveway and I guessed the parents were out for the night. I wondered if they knew about the party, or if their being out was the main reason it was being held.

'Whose party is it?' I tried. I'd been attempting conversation all the way here without any success. It had only been a twenty-minute walk from the snooker club, which wouldn't have been too bad if I'd been wearing shoes. Now my socks were soaked and my feet hurt. Blondie had trodden on my toes twice; accidentally on purpose, I guessed.

Trev had stayed to work behind the counter at The Angles, but everybody else was here, even Becky, and I'd tried to catch her eye a couple of times. She'd stuck close to Freddie. Or maybe he'd stuck close to her? I wasn't sure why she'd decided to speak up for me, although of course I was particularly grateful, and I knew even less of her boyfriend's reasons for agreeing. Once again I was the fly trapped in the spider's web.

Freddie seemed willing to talk now, however. 'Don't know his name,' he replied.

'He's not a friend, then?' I said. 'Are you sure he won't mind me tagging along? I'd hate to be a gate-crasher.'

'Don't worry,' he told me. 'We're all gate-crashers. But that's why we're here – it was rude not to invite us.' He smiled at my confusion. 'I was telling you about how we provide services? Well, party security is one of them.'

'Party security? As in bouncers?'

'Yeah, if you like.' He turned to Big George. 'Let them know we're here, will you?'

Freddie stayed on the road while Big George led Blondie, Hutty and Spike up to the front door. I realized this was the Tailor's hierarchy in action – or rather Freddie delegating the dirty work. Big George knocked politely on the door, and when it opened the other three barged inside.

'It's risky holding a party without security,' Freddie was saying. 'You can get all kinds of undesirables turning up. When drink and stuff's involved things have a nasty way of getting out of hand.'

'It's a protection racket,' I said, surprised by the hint of admiration that crept into my voice. 'If they don't pay you "security" money, you trash the place.'

'Go and join the fun,' Freddie told me.

I shook my head. 'I'm having plenty already, thanks.'

'Take him to enjoy the fun, Becky,' he said. 'He wants to be a Tailor, let him have fun like one.'

She took my hand and virtually skipped as she led me up the garden path.

We stepped through the front door. The music was still playing, but nobody seemed to be enjoying themselves – except for the Tailors.

Year Ten kids stood looking awkward and nervous, shuffling feet, not meeting eyes. Big George stayed in the hallway to make sure no one could escape. In the living room there were empty bottles of alcopop scattered around the floor, and a few half-hearted balloons that were slowly deflating. I could smell the distinct warm smoke from cannabis; there were a few empty beer cans being used as ashtrays. I noticed the room appeared strangely empty, or blank, and realized that whoever's house it was had had the foresight to tuck most of the ornaments away. Which felt like too little too late with the Tailors here.

Spike was making himself comfortable on the settee in between a couple who had probably been kissing only moments before. He snatched an unopened lager, threw it to Hutty. He put his arm round the girl's shoulders and his feet up on the coffee table. 'Come on!' he cried. 'Where the hell's this party?'

None of the Year Ten kids seemed to know.

So Hutty shouted, 'It's right here!' and shook the lager until it frothed and sprayed across the walls and carpet.

'Whey-hey!' Spike cried, kicking over the coffee table.

Becky tugged on my hand. 'Let's go see if anything interesting is happening upstairs.'

I followed because I couldn't bear to see what the Tailors were going to do. I knew it wasn't going to be pleasant. And as if proof were needed, as we passed down the hall to the stairs, I could hear Blondie in the kitchen saying, 'Your party? What do you mean *your* party? You don't get to have a party unless *we* say so!' I didn't see the look on the face of the kid he was talking to, but then again I doubted I really needed to.

'What the hell are you doing getting involved with this?' I asked Becky as she led me up the stairs.

'Freddie's my boyfriend,' she told me over her shoulder. Then, when we stepped onto the landing, she considered the doors and said, 'I like being nosey in other people's houses, don't you?'

'I'm not hanging around here. I'm going,' I said.

She gripped my hand tightly. 'You can't.'

'Watch me.'

She was shaking her head. 'You can't, that's not fair. If you go Freddie will blame me. I did you a favour, now you can do me one back.'

'Favour? You call bringing me here and getting me involved in this a favour?'

'I stopped you from getting beaten up, didn't I?

'For which I'll be eternally grateful – I think.'

'See, I'm a lovely person deep down.'

I didn't dare ask how deep. 'So come on, why did you do it?'

She pretended to look thoughtful. 'Because I like you. And I like you because you make me laugh. And you make me laugh because you're funny.' She'd chosen a door and poked her head inside. 'This one looks interesting,' she said and dragged me inside.

It was a bedroom; she flicked on the light. It could have been the room of the kid who was throwing the party, and was untidy enough to be the kind of room that frustrated most mothers. The bed was unmade, the wardrobe door hung open to show clothes stuffed in the bottom. CDs, DVDs and videos were scattered across the floor both in and out of their boxes, forcing you to watch where you stepped. A dirty breakfast bowl sat on top of the portable TV. Becky was staring at the posters of flashy sports cars on the wall.

'I don't understand boys who do this,' she said. 'You don't do this, do you?'

'Do what?' I asked.

'Put up pictures of cars.' I shook my head, and Becky said, 'I could understand pictures of sexy women in their underwear, but not cars or motorbikes. I think all boys who enjoy looking at cars more than women should have their names put on a secret police file and be watched very carefully when they're older. Because it's not natural, is it?' She crouched down and started looking through the CDs on the floor, casting them all aside. 'I doubt we'll find anything to suit your retro tastes here, John Malarkey.'

I was uncomfortable in somebody else's room. I hated the thought of a stranger being able to rummage through my personal belongings in my room. I was also a little worried that if Becky found something of interest she might steal it. But I didn't believe that, I realized. She was nosey, just like she'd said; curious, gossipy, but not a thief.

She poked and prodded most things, looked in a couple of drawers and even went through a stack of schoolwork dumped in the corner. 'He's not doing very well in science,' she informed me.

'Yeah? Well, it's not my favourite subject either. Come on, Becky, let's—'

'But do you know what upsets me most of all?' She gestured around the room. 'No books. And I love reading. I wish Freddie would read. I bet you read, don't you? I can tell. That's why you're like you are, because you read good books.'

I had my back to her and was walking out onto the landing.

123

She said, 'I'm really looking forward to your mum's shop opening.' She may have seen me flinch, the way my shoulders tightened. 'I mean it,' she was saying. 'Honestly. We need a decent bookshop around here.'

I still had my back to her. 'I'll make sure you're a VIP customer,' I said. If Becky knew about my mum's shop, then so did the Tailors. Freddie Cloth knew far too much about me for my liking.

From downstairs the music suddenly blasted out at the highest possible volume. That'll please the neighbours, I thought. It went silent just as quickly. Then loud again, then silent. There was harsh laughter. Becky moved by me to another door. 'Come on.' She took my hand again and pulled me inside.

We were greeted by blurry, tipsy voices, irritated at being disturbed. When Becky switched on the light two confused and embarrassed Year Tens squinted up from a fumble of sheets and ruffled clothes. Becky tutted at them and held the door open, looking like a disgruntled older sister. 'Out,' she ordered. They were quick to disappear. They probably knew who she was, who her boyfriend was. Then she closed the door and grinned at me.

It was the parents' bedroom, with pastel wallpaper and a thick carpet. The curtains were a bit too flowery for my taste; Becky's too. She sniffed disapprovingly. 'Might have been nice ten years ago,' she said. 'I want to be an interior designer, you know. I'm going to go to college to do a course.'

'Great,' I said. 'Fantastic. I'm pleased for you. But can you tell me what the bloody hell is going on here?'

'Freddie told us to have some fun.'

'And do you always do what Freddie tells you to?'

'He's my boyfriend.'

'So you keep saying. But I'm still trying to figure out why?'

She shrugged. 'He's—'

'A thug, a bully, a head-case?'

She ignored me. 'He's the first boyfriend I've ever had. My dad's really strict and he doesn't like me seeing boys very much. He wanted me to go to an all-girls' school!' The look on her face was proof enough of how appalling a thought this was for her.

'But he's okay with Freddie?' I asked.

She didn't answer; giving me the impression that Mr Chase wasn't told what his daughter considered he didn't need to know.

Eventually she said, 'I think Freddie's cute. And he's very strong. He tells me he loves me.'

'And do you believe him?'

Again Becky ignored the question. 'He's the most important person at school, and everybody knows I'm his girlfriend. Which means I'm important too.'

'You could be anybody's girlfriend.' I didn't need to add because she was beautiful.

A slow smile appeared on her lips. 'I could even be yours,' she said. 'Do you know that some of my friends fancy you? Carly and Marie who sit behind you in English? They think you're cute too. They'd be dead jealous if they knew we were alone in a bedroom together.'

'And what about Freddie? Do you reckon he'd be jealous as well? Or murderous perhaps? Maybe he'd want to do more than just give me a few bruises.'

She pursed her lips and tutted gently. Stepping closer, she stroked the bruising on my face. 'It does look painful.'

She licked her finger and rubbed the blue chalk mark from the tip of my nose. She knew how close she was to me. She knew the exact distance between us. Our eyes locked, but it was me who took a step back. 'I thought Freddie was being cruel,' she said.

'Join the club. So, do you know why he brought me along or not? Do you really think he believes I want to be in his gang?'

She laughed quickly. 'No! And anyway, he'd never really let you join.'

'So why's he brought me here?' I asked, but was wondering if it was a way of boasting, a show of strength of the Tailors. 'Didn't he tell you what was going to happen?'

'He never tells me anything – unless it's telling me what to do.'

'And you always do it. Because he's your boyfriend.'

She had a way of ignoring whatever she didn't like. She moved to open the large double wardrobe and poke her nose inside.

'I just want to know what's going on,' I said. 'You might enjoy being one of Freddie's puppets, but I'm not—'

She leaped back from the wardrobe and slammed the door hard enough to make the whole thing shudder. The look she gave me could have made my hair go crispy. 'I'm not *anybody's* puppet.' She regained her composure quick enough, however, and turned to leave. 'You don't know me at all,' she said. She walked out onto the landing. 'Stay here. If I can find out what's happening, maybe I'll let you know. Maybe Freddie will tell me what he wants you to do.'

She left me alone in the strange bedroom. I didn't

have much choice and could only wait for her to come back. I did consider trying to sneak out, and even went so far as checking the window. It looked like a long way down to the darkened back garden, however, and even then there was a high fence to scale at the bottom. All without shoes. So I waited.

Becky confused me. Had she been flirting with me? And if so, had Freddie put her up to it? My problem was how much I liked her. There was something about her that I couldn't quite put my finger on, but I was becoming worryingly smitten. Worryingly because I knew I didn't trust her. Worse, there were times when she seemed as dangerous as Cloth.

But maybe that was why I liked her?

I waited exactly as she'd told me to, and within a few minutes the noise and voices quietened downstairs. I listened at the door – not that I could make anything out. I felt sorry for whoever had thrown this misguided party: going by the look of the parents' room they liked things to be neat and well ordered, clean and tidy in this household. Which was the last thing it was going to be after the Tailors had finished.

I was going to have to take my chances getting away from Freddie and his gang once we were outside again. They'd had their fun with me, proved their muscle and shown just the way they worked. I was hoping it would be enough and they'd let me find my own way home. If not I was willing to run – I'd have to run – shoes or no shoes. I reckoned there should be plenty of opportunities to make a break for it when we were back out on the street.

Maybe as long as ten minutes passed. I was worried, anxious, fidgety.

I couldn't wait any longer and was ready to sneak out onto the landing to see what I could see. It seemed especially quiet downstairs now. Which was when I heard the police banging on the front door. And then it struck home what Freddie's plan had been all along. He'd probably even been the one to dial 999.

There wouldn't be a Tailor for at least a couple of miles by now; they'd be long gone. But upstairs was the dumb mug they'd dumped to take the blame, because all the Year Tens had seen me with them. I cursed Becky, for the bait that she was — unwitting or not.

I heard strong coppers' voices at the foot of the stairs. I went out the window.

TWELVE

Cars blew by in the dark, whipping up the icy rain, tyres hissing on the wet road. The night was as miserable as I felt. My feet had been killing me; now I was grateful they'd eventually numbed and I could easily pretend they were blocks of wood nailed to my ankles. The cuffs of my jeans were too long without a shoe's sole and trailed in the puddles, soaking up the water and becoming stiff all the way up to my knees. I was hunched and shivering against the black blanket of the sky. But the late-night garage's lights burned brightly.

I only had a fiver on me, stuffed in my back pocket, which I knew was enough for a taxi, but . . .

I think I'd twisted my ankle when I'd jumped/fallen out of that bedroom window. I'd certainly gone off patios – what was wrong with people having soft grass out the back these days? My coat had snagged and ripped getting over the fence at the bottom of the garden. I'd been lost in a suburban tangle of streets which all seemed to lead nowhere or double-back on themselves. I'd had to hide from cars because one might be the coppers, and wandering around without shoes might strike them as kind of suspicious. It was like a miracle when, getting on for an hour later and completely by accident, I'd found the cinema on the High Street and could at last work out which way was home.

Things had changed tonight. I still wanted to prove my innocence: yes, of course. It was just that revenge was sounding pretty bloody good too right now. I was worried and angry about the whole day being over, and that I was getting closer and closer to Mr Coleburn's deadline, yet I was even worse off than I'd been in the very beginning.

The garage forecourt was brighter than a sunny day, but the light was neon and harsh. The smell of petrol lingered even as the rain tried to wash it away. I was glad there were no cars filling up, no one to see me who by chance might recognize me. I shuffled between the pumps and tugged once, twice at the shop's heavy glass door before I realized it was locked.

The attendant working late was watching from behind his secure counter. His voice came electronically through a speaker I couldn't see. 'You'll have to use the night-window.'

I reckoned he saw more than his fair share of freaks and weirdos on the graveyard shift, so a tattered and torn, black-and-blue-faced kid with no shoes out in the rain was probably small-fry for him. He'd have better stories than me to tell to his mates in the pub. But I did wonder if he could operate the door's lock from behind his counter, and had decided I wasn't worth the risk.

I stepped up to the night-window and tried to smile, but it hurt my face too much. The attendant was watching me carefully. He was older than me – maybe a student, just topping up his loan.

'I've had a shit night,' I told him. I was walking on the spot because it seemed to help my feet if I kept them moving. 'Shit day, actually. All day's just been really bloody awful.'

He nodded, but I don't think he cared. 'What can I get you?' he asked.

'Twenty Marlboro Lights, please.' And I pushed my crumpled fiver through the gap underneath the security glass.

It felt like only one in a long list of failures today.

DESPERATE HOURS

THIRTEEN

Friday morning, the cloakroom was packed and noisy. I was waiting by Simon Penn's locker.

When I'd finally crawled into bed, after avoiding my mum and bathing my cut feet in perhaps a gallon or more of TCP, I'd lain awake for a long time staring up at the ceiling, thinking. Did it really matter if I got kicked out of school and wasn't able to take my exams? Did I really care? I could work downstairs with Mum; I didn't need qualifications to do that. Like Freddie had said, I wasn't one of them. I only had a couple of months left at Brook anyway, so why not let Freddie Cloth and the Tailors have the place all to themselves?

But deep down I knew I had way too much pride for that.

I wanted some kind of revenge.

I'd been loath to even set foot inside Brook again, and felt claustrophobic and paranoid the second I did. I'd come straight to the lockers to wait for Simon Penn, and couldn't stop myself from checking my watch several times in the space of only a few minutes. It obviously didn't help, but I was feeling a real pressure from the clock now – from Mr Coleburn's fast approaching deadline. I needed Simon to tell me everything he knew about the Tailors, and about this afternoon's football match. That football match was when my time would be up. Mr Coleburn could not wait beyond then: he'd be forced to admit what had happened, getting himself a reprimand and me an exclusion. Time was running out. I was relying on Simon for some nugget of information that would give me the kind of opportunity I so desperately needed.

I kept my eyes and ears open for any sign of Mr Macallan or Mr Coleburn, and watched the other students milling around. They seemed more boisterous than yesterday, but it was sunny outside, a Friday too, and was therefore another whole week closer to the Easter holidays. I wondered how many of them had been on the receiving end of Freddie Cloth and his gang.

There were only a couple of minutes to go before registration and I almost didn't spot Simon in the crowd. I just saw this kid suddenly turn round and hurry away in the opposite direction. I recognized the bad haircut and crap shoes. He'd obviously seen me and, still thinking I was a Tailor after seeing me at The Angles, decided it was best to stay clear. I hurried after him.

'Simon. Hey, Simon.' I blocked his way. He tried to walk past me but I wouldn't let him.

He looked pale and tired, grey bags under his eyes. I reckoned I wasn't the only one who wasn't getting much sleep at the moment. 'Leave me alone, can't you?'

'Listen, Simon – last night, it's not what you think.' I was pointing down at my feet, at my favourite pair of Converse.

He snorted at me through his nose, making a grumpy, childish sound. 'Wow, different trainers. Great.'

'I'm not a Tailor.'

'So why were you there last night? Why were you with Becky Chase?'

I tried to roll my eyes and smile in a You-wouldn't-believe-it! kind of way. 'Long story,' I said.

'I bet it is.' He sounded like a petulant nine-year-old, which was particularly annoying.

'I need to talk to you,' I said. 'Come on, let's go find somewhere quiet.'

'It's registration,' he told me.

I shrugged.

'I'm not skipping registration. And I've got nothing to say to you.'

'Listen, Simon—' But the bell sounded and everybody was on the move, jostling and pushing by me. I lost him in the hasty scrimmage.

In a matter of seconds I was the only person left standing in the corridor; classroom doors slammed, then the school was suddenly hushed. There was no way I'd be making an appearance in my own form room today, and I had to retreat to the toilets to keep out of sight.

It didn't matter too much because I knew which room 11B were in, but it was wasting time. I was impatient. I paced up and down in the toilets, checking my watch. When Mr Coleburn's Tannoy announcement for me to go to his office cut through the silence my nerves almost snapped.

'Would John Malarkey of Eleven C go to Mr Coleburn's office straight away. Mr Coleburn wants to see John Malarkey immediately.' He'd really be gunning for me today, no doubt about that.

I forced myself to wait five minutes. By now the register must have been taken and the notices read, I told myself. Then I went straight to 11B's form room and knocked at the door.

Mrs Lang called for me to come in. 'Mr Coleburn would like to see Simon Penn in his office,' I said.

The old teacher looked over the top of her glasses at her class. 'Simon? Was that your name on the Tannoy?'

All eyes in the room went to him.

'No, miss,' I told her. 'It was mine. But I've been asked to bring Simon along too.'

Mrs Lang was curious. She raised her eyebrows at Simon. 'You'd better hurry up then, hadn't you?' she said to him. 'Come along.'

He stayed where he was, looking shocked and maybe a little angry too. I willed him not to say anything, to just get up and walk out with me. But he wasn't the only one staring at me. Blondie and Big George were sitting next to each other towards the back of the class.

'Hey, Ev. Hiya, George,' I called, waving. Everybody was looking at me now. 'Good night last night, wasn't it?' I pointed at the bruise on my cheek. They could do nothing but glare at me.

Mrs Lang cleared her throat to let me know she wasn't impressed. Then: 'Move along there, Simon. Mr Coleburn will not be happy if you keep him waiting.'

Reluctantly he picked up his bag and followed me out into the corridor. I said thank you to the teacher, winked at the two Tailors, and closed the door. Simon was already stalking away up the corridor.

'Simon. Wait. Where're you running off to?'

'Are you purposely trying to get me into trouble?' he hissed.

'No, I'm trying to get me out of it. Come on.' I dragged him into the toilets.

Once inside he threw his bag down on the floor and stood with his hands on his hips, wanting to appear defiant but missing by a mile. 'What do you want?' he yelled, his high-pitched voice ringing around the walls. 'Why can't you just leave me alone?'

'Calm down, okay? I need your help.'

'How do I know you're not one of them?'

'Because they gave me this,' I said, turning so he could see my cheek. 'If you can remember, I didn't have it when you left last night.'

'Why were you wearing their trainers?'

'I stole them. I wanted to rile them up a bit, and I guess I managed it a little too well for my own good.'

He wasn't sure whether he believed me or not.

'Look, I'm in really big trouble because of them. I'm the one Mr Coleburn thinks stole the report cards, and I'm the one he's trying to expel.'

'Why?'

'Because the Tailors set me up. This isn't a story, Simon. I swear, okay? All I want to do is not get kicked out, by proving to Coleburn it wasn't me.'

I was getting him on my side. He dropped his hands off his hips, relaxing. 'I don't see what it's got to do with me. I'm not sure I can do anything about it.'

'I just need you to tell me about them.'

He shrugged. 'What do you mean?'

'When did they get together?'

'I heard they started out in Year Nine by just doing stupid dares, like setting off fire alarms and stuff, or by sneaking onto the roof. Once they broke into the trophy cabinet in the hall and peed in all the sports cups. It wasn't until last year that they took over the tuck shop, and then started doing the other stuff too.'

'What other stuff? How do they make money?'

'They sell cigarettes.'

'Yeah, I know.' I was impatient. 'The tuck shop, you just said.'

He nodded. 'And drink. And drugs. Well, *joints* anyway.'

So that was what they'd been expecting me to buy yesterday when I'd been asked, 'What else?' over and over again. And I wondered if they'd been the ones to sell the stuff for the Year Tens' party last night, even though they knew they were going to crash it.

'Remember you told me something about a homework club?' I asked Simon. 'What was that?'

He still looked uncertain; he chewed on his bottom lip. 'The Tailors run it,' he said eventually. 'I have to do other people's homework for them.'

I nodded, trying to encourage him. 'Okay. And?'

'And nothing. That's it.'

'Yeah, but how's it work exactly? Why do you do all that work for other people?'

'They force me.'

'Do they beat you up?'

He shook his head. 'It's blackmail.'

I nodded again, trying to be patient. 'Okay.'

He let out a big sigh, and at last started to talk openly. 'George Cullum? From my class?' I was still nodding: Big George. 'He came up to me last year, saying they'd pay me if I did a bit of his homework for him. Just a history essay. He said he'd give me five pounds, so I said okay.'

'But he didn't pay you,' I guessed.

'No, no. He paid me. But he came back the next week with more homework and said he'd give me ten pounds if I did that. So I did, but this time he didn't pay me. He said he'd pay me next time, and just kept giving me more and more work to do, always saying next time he'd pay me. I tried arguing, but he started threatening to tell the teachers about me doing it for money the first time.'

'You have tried to stop though, yeah?'

He nodded. 'But they didn't go to the teachers. They stole my little brother's bag. He's in Year Eight, and they stole his bag so he was the one who got into trouble for not being able to hand his own homework in.'

'They've got a habit of stealing bags,' I said. 'So they force you to do the work or they'll bully your little brother?'

Simon's miserable face said it all. 'They slashed the tyres on his bike when I didn't do this one assignment properly. You always have to get a "C" or above or they do something.'

I remembered what Freddie Cloth had told me last night about the Tailors providing a service for the students at Brook. 'It's called the Homework *Club*,' I said. 'So that means you're not the only one, are you?'

'We're not meant to talk about it – you get threatened not to tell anybody if you're a member. But I know two others who are doing the same as me. Maybe a few more as well. I think there's a boy in your class too.'

'There must be a whole network of geeks and boffins doing other people's assignments.'

He didn't seem at all offended by being labelled as such; he'd probably heard it all before anyway. 'But I can't do all the work they give me as well as my own,' he whined. 'I'm behind in maths and science.'

'Which is why even you needed a stolen report card.'

'I haven't written it yet,' he said quickly. 'It's still in my locker.'

I wasn't really listening to him. In my mind the idea of somehow breaking up the Homework Club sounded like a good one. Not that I had any kind of clue how to do it.

'How do you get the work back to the Tailors? Do they collect it from you personally?' I was thinking of Simon sharing his form room with Blondie and Big George.

'They have a box in the library.'

I frowned at this. 'I don't . . .'

'The teachers all have assignment collection boxes in the library, for when you hand work in on deadline days. You give it to Mrs Wright, the librarian, and have to sign your name. The Homework Club hand work in to a box for "Mr Tailor".'

'And there is no Mr Tailor at Brook.'

Simon shook his head.

I had to smile. 'But there are so many teachers that the librarian hasn't noticed she's never met this one in particular.' I hated myself for feeling more and more impressed with Freddie Cloth's operation. Maybe he was right, after all. Maybe he really was as clever as he made out. I just hoped I could be cleverer before this afternoon.

That reminded me. 'Tell me about this football match,' I said suddenly.

'What about it?' Simon asked.

'It's a final or something, right?'

'I don't know much about football.'

'You know about this match, though, yeah? Everybody's got the afternoon off, haven't they?'

'We have, because it's the Year Eleven final against Stonner Secondary, and I don't think we've ever been in the final of anything before. It's supposed to be a special treat. Mr Coleburn says that everybody's got to watch it.' Simon looked less than pleased with the idea.

'Where can I bet on it? The Tailors are taking bets, aren't they?'

'The tuck shop, probably. Or there's usually one of them round the back of the drama hall.'

The smokers' lair. 'What're the odds?'

He didn't have a clue. 'But it's Stonner Secondary,' he said as though this meant something important.

'What about them?'

'The Homework Club is doing work for them too.'

'Eh? Run that by me one more time.'

'It's GCSE coursework. I've done essays for other schools too. That's why I'm so behind. But I've still got stuff to do for Stonner.' He looked paler than ever; anxious and over-tired.

The bell rang: first period. There was noise out in the corridor again. My mind was working quickly, trying to sort all this information into some kind of order I could use.

Simon was still talking; didn't seem to be in a rush to get to his lesson any more. 'I tried telling Freddie last night – I haven't been able to finish all of it. He said that if I didn't have it in time for the football match he'd make me regret it. What do you think he'll do?'

'I don't know,' I said. Then: 'But if he wants it for today, for the match, then that must be when he's planning on handing it over. He must be meeting someone from Stonner who's collecting it. Not that that really helps me much.' I wasn't talking to Simon, just speaking my thoughts out loud.

A group of three lads came in, banging open the door, talking loudly. They didn't take much notice of us as they headed for the urinals.

Simon lowered his voice to ask, 'Are you going to help us?'

I was confused. 'Help who? What do you mean?'

'Help the Homework Club. Stop it or something.'

'I'm sorry, Simon,' I said. 'But I'm only out to help myself at the minute. I'm the one with all the grief here, remember?'

'So am I.'

I shook my head. 'So do something about it. I'm too busy dragging my own backside out of the fire. I can't—'

Simon snatched his bag up from the floor. 'I'm going to fail my GCSEs,' he shouted.

The three lads looked round at us. I held up my hands to quieten Simon down. 'And I'm going to get kicked out before I can even take them.'

'So we've both got the same *grief*, haven't we?' he yelled.

I didn't have an answer, and he pushed past me, slamming out through the door.

FOURTEEN

Of course I was sympathetic to Simon's problems, and to the rest of the Homework Club too, whoever they might be. But it was myself I was worried about. The last thing I needed right now was him trying to give me some kind of moral quest. If I'd learned anything yesterday, it was that Brook High was no place for a conscience.

Again I waited for the school to settle, for the lessons to get under way behind closed classroom doors, then I headed upstairs to the library.

My biggest concern right now was that the librarian, Mrs Wright, could recognize me. I stepped just inside the door and hovered, ready to run if I needed to. She looked up from where she was sorting books at her desk, but it seemed that for once my luck was going to hold. She returned to her work without a second glance. I reckoned I should be thankful for the number of students she had to deal with in a single day.

There were a few other kids poring over the shelves, or sitting at a desk with chunky reference books open between them. Everybody was hushed. Except for a group of Year Eight lads, who were huddled around talking and giggling. Mrs Wright tutted warnings in their direction at regular intervals.

It was a long, thin room, divided in two with the bookshelves at one end and the desks at the other. There were only a couple of computers because students were encouraged to use the new IT suite in Top Block. Which I'd heard had pleased Mrs Wright immensely, seeing as she wasn't a fan of computers. Her desk was more or less central on the far side of the room. Behind her was a rack of wooden 'pigeonholes' with cardboard boxes inside, and written on the fronts of these boxes were teachers' names. These were the assignment collection boxes.

I got one of the younger kids at a desk to lend me a few sheets of A4. On the top sheet I wrote my name and form, and 'Mr Tailor', made it look as much like an assignment as possible. On the three sheets underneath I wrote: 'Freddie Cloth . . . is . . . an arsehole.' It was petty and childish, but it made me smile.

I took the pages over to Mrs Wright. 'Can I hand this in to Mr Tailor's box, please?'

She reached behind her and took down the fullest, heaviest cardboard box from the pigeonholes. 'It certainly looks like he's got a busy weekend of marking ahead of him, doesn't it?' she said. She got me to fill in my name and the date and time on a form to prove I'd handed the work in, then replaced the box.

'Thank you,' I said.

She smiled at me. 'You're welcome.' She looked as though she knew my face, just wasn't able to place it. I supposed it was the same for her with a lot of the students.

So, I knew about the Homework Club, and about how the Tailors were using it to spread their influence to other schools, but it didn't get me any closer to proving my innocence. I knew about fixing the football match, about selling the report cards. But did any of this wonderful knowledge help me to prove my innocence? Somehow I doubted it.

I grabbed a random book from the nearest shelf and sat down at one of the desks. I needed a plan. I held the book open in front of me, but stared right through the words on the page as if they weren't there.

Come on, I told myself. Think. How long until this afternoon's football match?

I checked my watch.

Not long enough, obviously.

All I could think about, however, was how upset my mum was going to be. I'd managed to hide my bruising from her this morning, but she was bound to see it sometime over the weekend. Maybe I should be trying to come up with an explanation for her? She was so excited about her bookshop, and I didn't want to be the one who brought worry and disappointment.

I got up to wander between the shelves, looking for any kind of inspiration, anywhere. I wandered through fiction and non-fiction, but I wasn't really looking at the books. My mind felt like it was running through an ever-frustrating maze — dead end after dead end after dead end. I was getting angry with myself. I couldn't let Cloth do this to me.

And time was slipping by, running out.

I decided to leave, but had to duck back behind the shelves when I spotted Blondie hanging about just outside the door.

My first thought was that he knew I was here. I'd been seen, the Tailors had been told, and they were all gathering outside to snare me. But when he came inside I saw the clutch of papers he had in his hand and realized he must be on collection duty for the Homework Club, mopping up any stray assignments before this afternoon's handover, not trusting them to get the work completed unless there were some strong-arm tactics employed. Probably being extra vigilant because of how important to the Tailors their dealings with Stonner Secondary must be. Or maybe because of me. He walked straight up to Mrs Wright's desk.

I turned my back on him, really studying the books on the shelves now, not wanting to be seen. And suddenly saw my number on the spine of a large textbook.

574.1.

I dug in three different pockets before I found the scrap of paper I'd bought off Grunter. But there it was: '574.1'. And there it was on the spine of some kind of biology book.

I heard Blondie saying, 'I've got some assignments to hand in for Mr Tailor.'

And the librarian exclaimed, 'More? My goodness, he certainly is going to be a busy man, isn't he?'

Making sure I had a fully stacked shelf between them and me, I started flipping through the pages. I was impatient to find something important. Why on earth would anybody want to buy the number of a biology reference book? A ripped page fell out and fluttered to the floor. I kept my eye on Blondie through the shelf as I bent down quickly to retrieve it. A little part of me was concerned Mrs Wright might think I'd damaged the book myself, but it wasn't a page from this particular book I was holding, although perhaps it could loosely be termed as biology.

It was a page from a porn mag. A glossy, pouting and completely naked woman stared up at me. On the reverse side she was joined by what I assumed was a close friend.

I was quick to put it back exactly as I'd found it. I'd

only paid two quid for this, but I could have handed over a fiver. I wondered what you got for the higher price. And then I began to wonder just how many of these books had extra pages slipped inside. I also cast a glance over at the huddled, giggling Year Eight boys crowded around one of the desks. Mrs Wright would go ballistic if she knew what they were really using her library for.

Maybe I should tell her? But I didn't think it would do me any good. I couldn't prove Freddie Cloth and the Tailors had anything to do with it.

Blondie was signing and dating the form from Mr Tailor's collection box, and I saw his hand pause and hover for one second, then two. He was reading my name, today's date, and the time – about five minutes ago. I saw his face darken. He looked around the library, eyes narrowed. He spotted me easily enough.

He wasn't sure what to do. I guessed by the look of him he wanted to punch me very hard, but he knew he couldn't do it here. I thought he might just ignore me and walk away, but the temptation must have been too strong because he made his mind up and came over.

'I heard you had a run-in with the police at that party,' he smirked, thinking he was funny.

'It was a nice try,' I admitted. 'But not quite. Tell Freddie his little plan failed.'

'You got off lightly. But now you know not to mess with us.'

I shrugged. I didn't like being told what to do by this goon.

'You're not Brook, you're not a Tailor – you're nothing,' he told me.

His tone of voice was rubbing me the wrong way. We stood square to each other, eye to eye. 'Why don't you shut your mouth?'

'Why don't you make me?'

I pulled the biology book from the shelf and shoved the page from the porn mag under his nose. 'Why don't I let Mrs Wright know how and where I got this?'

He was quick to snatch the page from me and stuff it into his pocket. 'Just keep out of our business, Malarkey,' he growled. 'You must have a death wish or something. What do you want written on your gravestone?'

'How about: "He died peacefully in his sleep aged eighty-three"?'

He curled his lip at me. 'Outside,' he hissed in my ear. 'Now!'

I let him steer me towards the door and out into the empty corridor. He pushed me up against the wall hard enough to make my teeth rattle.

'You just won't give in and piss off, will you? Wasn't last night enough for you?'

I shoved his hand away, stood my ground. 'I hate backing down,' I told him.

'Let's see what Freddie has to say about it.' He fished in his jacket and brought out a mobile phone. But it wasn't the right one, because he pulled a smaller, trendier model out of an inside pocket, which he flipped open to dial single-handedly.

My mind was quick to join the dots. 'So you're the one with the goalie's mobile,' I said, nodding at the spare one he was carrying.

He didn't say anything, just hurriedly tried to stuff it back in his pocket. But it was all the answer I needed.

I tried to snatch it from him, couldn't get a proper grip on it, only managed to knock it out of his hand. It hit the floor and spun and skittered away.

We both made a dive for it at the same time, cracking skulls, tumbling over each other. The Tailor grunted in unexpected pain. I was on my knees, scurrying along after the mobile. He grabbed my ankle, pulled me back. I kicked out at him with no effect.

He dragged me on my knees away from where the phone lay, my hands scrabbling on the floor. The toe of the trainer on my free foot squealed on the tiles. But as soon as he let go of me, trying to get past me, I was lunging forward again. And this time I got my fingers on it, and wrapped them round tight.

'Give it here, you little prick!'

I wrestled in his grip. He was bigger than me, stronger than me. He had my wrist, twisting up my skin painfully, digging his nails in, trying to make me drop the phone again. I had his wrist, was forcing it back on itself. We stumbled against each other, back and forth across the corridor. I wasn't going to beat him in a fair fight, I knew that. So I brought my foot down on his shin, scraping hard down the length of his ankle to his foot, and stomped on it with all my might. He howled and had to step away. With a sudden wrench I got free and was running.

I held onto that phone like I was never going to let go of it again and thundered down the corridor. He was slow to come after me; I must have caught his shin and ankle just right. I was up one set of stairs, down the next. The Tailor couldn't keep up. He was hobbling badly.

I flew outside and across the Quad, not caring who

was looking, who saw me. I doubled back on myself around the science block. Then again the other way. I ran into the first open door I saw, along the corridor to the closest toilets, barged into a cubicle and locked the door.

My heart hammered at my ribcage, almost alarmingly so. Don't give up on me now, I was thinking. Not now. I shuddered with gasping breaths. But *I* had the goalie's phone. *I* had something Freddie Cloth would be desperate to get back.

I closed my eyes and leaned my sweating forehead against the cubicle wall, waited for my heart rate to slow. It was thumping harder than a premature burial on the coffin lid.

I allowed myself the briefest of smiles and put the phone in my pocket. Now *I* had bargaining power.

I just hoped there was time enough to use it.

FIFTEEN

The phone was a fairly chunky black thing that had probably gone out of fashion within a couple of months of Davie the goalkeeper buying it. It was, however, something I knew Freddie Cloth was going to be desperate to get his hands on. And if I stayed cool, if I played my cards right . . .

It came to life suddenly in my hand. The little rectangular screen lit up green, displaying the caller's number, while the ring tone itself was shrill and piercing. I covered the tiny speaker with the pad of my thumb to muffle the sound and let it ring. Although I didn't recognize the number displayed it didn't take a genius to guess who was calling. The ringing stopped when the voice messaging service kicked in, but I kept my thumb pressed over the speaker, knowing that almost immediately it would start ringing again.

And when it did, I answered.

I sounded cheerful, full of fun. 'Hey, Freddie!'

'Malarkey.' His voice sounded strained, breathy. I could hear heavy footsteps in the background and guessed he was on the move.

'How's my favourite low-life scum?' I asked.

'I want that phone.'

'Yeah, I thought you might,' I said, and cut him off. I waited for a count of ten seconds and then the phone rang again. 'Hi, Freddie.'

'You wouldn't believe how much you're getting on my nerves right now, Malarkey.'

'I reckon I could take an educated guess,' I told him, thinking it sounded like he was running.

'Don't forget what happened last night . . .' he threatened.

'The coppers didn't get me,' I said.

'Pity,' he replied.

'Not that it matters, because I'm the one in control now.'

'Give me that phone back, you piece of sh—!'

Again, I killed the call.

I only managed to count to five this time. As soon as I answered I repeated, 'I'm in control now, Freddie. I could give this phone back to Davie any time I please. And if Davie has his phone back, all bets would be off, right? Wouldn't that be a terrible thing to happen, eh?'

'You reckon, do you?' He'd stopped running and sounded a little out of breath.

Where are you, Freddie? I was thinking. Where are you looking for me? What I said out loud, however, was: 'I could let Davie know he's safe any time I please. And I'd tell him to save as many goals as he likes. "Yay, Brook! Brook to win the cup!" That's what I'd say.'

'We'll tear the school down brick by brick to find you if we have to.'

'Maybe I'm not in school any more.'

'Oh, I think you are. We'll find you.'

'I'm long gone,' I tried, really wanting him to believe I was off school grounds. Then: 'But I am willing to do you a deal, Freddie. You can have this phone, okay – I'll let you have it back, if you'll do something for me in return.'

'And what would that be?'

'Guess.'

'I'm warning you, Malarkey . . .'

'In return, I want Coleburn off my back. I want you to send one of your minions to him – a sacrifice, if you like – to take the fall for stealing the report cards.'

He laughed at me. 'Yeah, like that's going to happen in this lifetime.'

'That's the deal,' I said. 'That's the only way you're going to get this phone back.'

'We'll get it back.'

I let his words hang in the air unanswered as I got to my feet and got myself moving. Out of the toilets, along the science block corridor, sneaking past the labs. The problem was, I believed they could find me – *would* find me – unless I managed to stay one step ahead.

Cloth must have been able to hear me like I'd heard him. 'That's right, Malarkey,' his voice hissed in my ear. '*Run.*'

I didn't want to stay in the science block: it was too small, I could easily be cornered. I'd been reckless charging headlong into here, and was just plain lucky I'd not been seen, so I was now wary of disturbing the lessons going on in the labs. Quickly, quietly I sneaked along the corridor to the nearest door, past labs where lessons were in full flow with Bunsen burners and periodic tables.

The outside door led onto the Quad. I hid to one side of it and peered through the glass panel. I had a good view of the pathway leading straight ahead in front of me all the way to the main entrance, and the other paths leading to the main block and Top Block crossing over it. In between were grass borders and flowerbeds, and the willow tree some mayor or other had planted all those years ago when the school was first built. Over to my right would be the sixth-form common room, and on my left the bike sheds and the gates onto Raymond Avenue. Not that I could see these. If I wanted to be able to I'd have to stick my head out into the fresh air and I certainly wasn't willing to do that just yet. But I couldn't see Freddie or any of his friends either.

I realized I didn't know how many Tailors there were; I obviously hadn't met the whole happy family. They could be anywhere. I didn't doubt for a second that Cloth would drag as many as he could from their lessons to hunt me down. I remembered how I'd felt yesterday with Mr Macallan chasing me, and that feeling of having a net closing in on me was nothing compared to the certainty I felt now.

Or maybe it was a spider's web. I was the fly, right?

I was ready to get moving again, but before I did I went through the phone's memory, and deleted every number Davie had stored there. Even if Cloth did catch me, did get his hands on the phone, I reckoned it would be pretty much useless to him now.

I only had a few hours before Mr Coleburn would be forced to take action – to maybe make his threats of expulsion real. I needed somewhere to lay low for a while, long enough for Freddie to panic about the phone and go through with sending someone to Mr Coleburn to take the blame instead of me. I kind of hoped it would be Spike – I'd never forget the way he'd raised his foot above me.

There was no one outside that I could see, but it didn't necessarily mean there *wasn't* someone there, hiding, waiting. Did I dare make a run for it? Where are you, Freddie? I repeated in my head. Where are you looking for me?

Maybe I should head straight for the gates? Surely the further away from Brook I could get the better. But if I was going to bump into Tailors anywhere, I reckoned it would be at the gates. They'd have all three of them covered, not just Raymond Ave. The problem was I didn't want to be caught by teachers or Tailors. I needed some nook or cranny or hidey-hole, but the Tailors would probably know about every one of them: it was their business to know about the dark corners. So maybe I should leave the phone some place safe? It would make no difference if they got me then, not if I had the phone hidden somewhere safe. The question was, where was safe? Maybe I could leave it . . . ?

I saw someone crossing the Quad, and instantly flattened myself up against the wall. I twisted my head just far enough for one straining eye to see. It was the Tailor who worked at The Angles; he was coming my way.

I watched him, willing him to change paths, but he was definitely coming here, to this door, to where I was hiding, watching. And there was nowhere for me to go when he did. I was ready to sprint back to the toilets, even though I knew it was too obvious a place to hide – undoubtedly the first to be checked. Maybe I could take him, I was thinking; one on one. He'd been nervous of me last night, so maybe I could take advantage. But he'd already seen me. He was going for his mobile, calling for the others. He was running.

I ducked out of sight but stayed round the side of the doorway. I could hear him running, his black Adidas thudding on the path. He was shouting, 'He's here, he's here! The science block!' into his phone. The door slammed wide with a bang of its hinges as he charged inside. I kicked it back as hard as I could. I heard the crunch and was round the door ready to fight. But he was on the ground on his backside, holding his bloody nose and scrambling away from me.

I made as though I was going to lunge at him and he cowered with his hands over his head. 'Where's Freddie?' I asked.

'How should I know?'

I crouched down to face him and he tried to crawl away from me. There was a bubble of blood and snot at one of his nostrils. I held him by the crimson-stained front of his shirt. '*Where?*'

'The gym block,' he whimpered and the bubble popped.

I wiped my hand on his shoulder in disgust. He'd dropped his phone and I stamped on it twice, smashed it into the path before I took off again.

I didn't risk the open ground of the Quad and headed round the side of the science block, not really knowing where I was going, just as long as it was in the opposite direction to the gym block. There were at least half a dozen of the biscuit-tin variety of mobile classrooms and I tried to get myself lost in the middle of them. I followed the narrow paths cutting between them randomly in case anybody was following – they could have been leading me anywhere. In fact they led me to Big George.

I doubled back but he'd already seen me. I took the

first open door into the nearest block, along another corridor like a million others in this school. The Tailor was close behind but neither of us was running – not inside with lessons on the go. We were both wary of teacher interference and scurried past the classrooms as silently as we could. I was checking over my shoulder as the corridor turned left; there was an empty room. I ducked inside, hoping I was too quick for Big George to see. But no such luck. Immediately I realized my mistake, because now there was no way out and he had me well and truly trapped.

He closed the door after him and spoke into his mobile. 'I've got him . . . Yeah, one of the art rooms . . .' He laughed. 'No, don't worry. We're not going anywhere.'

The chunky wooden tables were psychedelically spattered and scored. There were paintings of bowls of misshapen fruit and bad portraits of ugly kids on the walls. I was backing myself into a corner, but at least I was keeping as far away from the Tailor as I could. He saw me eyeing up the window and said, 'Don't even think about it.'

'Come on, where's the fun in catching me?' I said. 'I thought the thrill was in the chase.'

Big George wasn't amused. 'I can't wait to see you get your smart mouth closed once and for all.' He stayed at the door, blocking my exit. 'Freddie's on his way. Why don't you give me that phone?'

I was stalling for time. If I was going to even get close to the window I had to scramble over a sink full of dirty paintbrushes in jam jars, up onto the windowsill lined with squeezy paint bottles, and only then would I find out if it was actually locked or not. I measured the distance between the Tailor and me and quite honestly didn't fancy my chances.

'Why's Freddie the boss?' I asked. 'How come you do everything he says? You're like those little fish allowed to swim around inside a shark's mouth to clean its teeth. You know that, don't you?'

'I'm going to *so* enjoy watching your mouth get shut for good. You'll be cleaning your teeth in a glass.'

The problem was, I believed him. If I didn't do something quick I was going to be a three-soups-a-day kind of person when Freddie arrived and realized I'd deleted the phone's memory. So I did the first thing that came to mind. I grabbed as many squeezy paint bottles as I could and hurled them at Big George.

They were the size and shape of old-fashioned washing-up liquid bottles, but felt heavy. The first one only missed him because he ducked, but it burst its thick yellow paint on the wall above his head as the top flew off. He howled as it spattered down on him. The second one, a blue one, hit his shoulder, making him cry out, but didn't open. The third had a helping hand from me unscrewing the top slightly before I threw it. It was a deep red, and when it exploded across his chest it was like a scene from a horror movie.

He was running at me now, coming round the tables to get at me. Which was his big mistake. I could keep hurling the bottles of paint at him, and could dodge around to the other side of the room. He should have stayed guarding the door. I was out into the corridor and didn't give a damn about disturbing lessons now. I flew past the classrooms and outside.

Back round the science block, out into the Quad at full pelt, heading for the main entrance. Big George was behind me; over my shoulder the one they called Hutty appeared; then Spike was there in front. I switched paths, jumping across the grass and flowerbeds, making for Top Block now. My heart was going quicker than my legs. I had a sliver of a lead, but Hutty was real close, too close, and Spike looked as though he might be able to cut me off.

The staff room sits on top of the main entrance. There was a sudden banging on the windows, and a teacher was bawling at us through the glass. None of us even glanced up. I knew that if they got their hands on me now I was dead meat. I was in control as long as I had the phone. I had to keep hold of the phone.

Somehow I managed to get to Top Block before Spike. I wrenched open the door and threw myself inside. I sprinted along the corridor. I didn't have a clue where I was going. Then suddenly a door to my left opened.

'Quick!' Becky Chase hissed, waving me frantically inside. 'Quick! In here.'

Did I trust her? I turned to look over my shoulder. Did I have much of a choice? The Tailors would be on me in a second like a pack of wolves. I pushed past her and she hurried the door closed behind me.

We were in the lecture theatre. There was a lectern, a microphone and a projection screen facing a steep tier of seats that rose up in front of us, similar to those in a normal theatre. I followed as Becky ran up the steps between the seats and we lay down on the floor between two of the rows, high up near the back. I was breathing hard, but I forced myself to take the breaths slowly, quietly. I didn't think Becky needed to lie quite as close to me as she was – pressing herself up against me, her mouth almost touching my ear – but I didn't say anything because the door I'd charged through only seconds before was opened.

I could hear Becky's breath in my ear. Then voices.

'Did you see him come in here?' It was Spike.

Big George replied, 'I didn't see where he went. Did he come in here? Did you see him?'

I imagined I could feel his eyes like the beam of a lighthouse sweep around and over us as we lay there.

'Shit!' Big George swore loudly. 'I *had* him! I had him and look what he did!'

Spike again: 'What happened? Is that paint?'

'I'm going to kill him!' George spat. 'He's dead!'

The bell to signal the end of the first period rang at exactly 9.45 and I could hear the corridor fill up with bustle and noise as everybody moved on to their next lesson.

'Freddie's going to be spitting feathers,' Spike told Big George. 'Come on, let's check outside. He'll head outside as soon as he gets the chance. He'll just want to get out of school as fast as possible.'

I didn't realize I'd been holding my breath until the door was slammed shut. Then it all came out in a rush. I tried to stand, but Becky held me down.

'They might come back,' she whispered.

I pushed her gently away and got to my feet. 'I doubt it, but thanks. Thanks for . . .' I wasn't sure how to put it. I went down between the seats to the door and listened. The corridor was settling down, a few doors slammed on full classrooms, cutting off any chatter. There was no sound of the Tailors sneaking about but I wasn't going to stick my head out just yet.

Becky had followed me. 'Do you mean thank you for saving you? Again?'

'Okay,' I said. 'For saving me. Again.' The problem was, I couldn't work out why. 'But where's the catch, Becky? When do you leave me and the police appear?'

'I didn't know that's what they were planning. I'm never told anything. It's true, I promise.'

I scoffed at her, then made a show of looking all around me, under chairs, up to the ceiling. 'When does your boyfriend jump out and punch me?'

She smiled, shrugged. 'Maybe I'm going off him. Maybe I like you instead.'

'O-kay,' I said slowly. 'And I should trust you because . . . ?'

But Becky was getting close again, taking hold of my hand, her eyes never leaving mine. 'You make me laugh. Isn't a good sense of humour what women want?'

'You believe that, do you?'

'Of course. I saw it written on a T-shirt.'

'*You're* the funny one,' I told her. 'You'll have to let me make notes sometime.'

'Any time.'

I realized that she was trying to get closer, and I was trying to back away. But all too soon she had me up against the wall. It was a bit too full-on for me. 'Listen, Becky, thanks and everything, but I really ought to get going before your boyfriend does manage to find me here.'

'Do you know how angry he'd be if he knew what I was doing?'

'That's kind of my point. I'd rather not be on the receiving end of—'

'I mean he'd be angry at *me*,' she said.

'So what are you doing here, then?'

'I told you. I like you.'

'And you don't like Freddie any more?' I asked. 'Last night you called me his puppet.'

'Sorry, but that's how it looks from the outside.'

She seemed to consider this. 'I was thinking about it. I'm more of an ornament. He likes me to look nice. He buys me expensive clothes. He says he does it because he loves me, but maybe it's because he loves the way he looks when he's with me and I'm wearing them.'

I wasn't going to say anything, but she turned to me as though she wanted confirmation. 'You'd probably look great if you were wearing a black bin bag,' I told her.

'That's why I like you, John Malarkey,' she said, smiling now. 'Because of the way you talk. Because of what you say. It proves how clever you are.' She was close enough for me to be able smell her shampoo. 'Freddie's not clever like that.' She touched the bruising on my cheek with the tips of her slim fingers. 'He's strong. But so are you. But in a different way to him. *You're* different to lots of people, aren't you? I think Freddie's only strong because he's mean. But I like the way you talk.' She rested her head on my shoulder. I could feel her breath on my neck. 'And I can tell you like things about me too.' She looked up at me. 'You do, don't you?'

I nodded. 'I like you,' I admitted. The problem was not knowing whether I could trust her.

She had her hands on my shoulders, then my chest. 'So what's he chasing you for now?'

She had me trapped; there was nowhere left for me to run. I wasn't sure whether I wanted to any more. 'I've got Davie the goalie's mobile.' She was beautiful. This was crazy.

'And you're going to give it back to him and spoil Freddie's little bets.'

I let her hold me. 'Let's just say I'm not keen on the idea of Freddie getting hold of it again.'

'Do you have it on you?' Her fingers were insinuating themselves inside my jacket – and suddenly the spell was broken.

I shoved her away. 'No,' I lied. 'It's somewhere safe. And thanks for the whole seduction and everything, but you're not having it either.'

She surprised me by looking genuinely offended. 'I don't care about some goalie's phone or Freddie's pathetic gang. I just think you're nice. I like you. I like you a lot.'

Was she genuinely offended, though? Or was she just a damn good actress? When she stepped up to me again, when she kissed me, I didn't stop her.

'You're very *different*,' she told me again.

'But your father might like me,' I said. 'Whereas I'm sure he hates Freddie.'

'What do I care what my dad thinks?' she replied a little too quickly. 'He doesn't even live with us any more and he still reckons he can tell us what to do. And I don't like *his* new girlfriend either. So we're even, aren't we?' She took a breath, then smiled slowly. 'He doesn't know half of what happens in my life anyway.'

'I'll bet,' I said.

I should have been looking at her face. I knew I should have been looking at her face. I told myself I should have been looking at her face. But I was staring at her fingers as they undid her blouse. They worked well together – slim, smooth, easing the buttons undone. She was wearing a black bra with a thin red trim around the edge. It wasn't a particularly subtle bra, but then Becky wasn't a particularly subtle girl.

And this was the school's lecture theatre!

I pushed her away one final time. 'You're going to get me into trouble.'

'Who's bothered about Freddie?'

'It's not just Freddie I'm worried about,' I said, thinking how great this would look if Mr Macallan or Mr Coleburn decided to poke their heads round the door. Then: 'I'll tell you where the phone is if you tell me about the Homework Club.'

'I don't care where the phone is.'

'But I want to know about the Homework Club. They've done a load of coursework for Stonner Secondary, right? Is Freddie handing it over at the match this afternoon?'

She seemed uninterested, but nodded all the same. 'After the match has finished. Freddie's going to give it to Jade's boyfriend in exchange for all the betting money. That's why Freddie sent us to Stonner to see him yesterday afternoon, so we could arrange it.'

'Freddie often get you working for him, does he?'

'I'm *not* his puppet! I hate it when you say that.' She was angry with me – then with him. 'I'm the one who'll be in trouble if I get caught. You never see *him* in the tuck shop, or doing the stealing or anything.'

'He's a clever lad,' I admitted, remembering the way he stayed clear of the party last night.

She snorted. 'Maybe.' She was resting her head on my shoulder. 'So where's the mobile?'

'I thought you didn't care?'

She shrugged.

'I've hidden it in Simon Penn's locker,' I lied. 'Do you know him? He's in Eleven B.'

She nodded. 'What did you hide it there for?'

'So Freddie won't find it.' Although deep down I got the feeling Simon Penn's locker would be ransacked within the hour.

'Do you trust me?' Becky asked suddenly. Then, when I hesitated to answer, 'Tell me, honestly − do you trust me?'

I lied again. 'I must do. I wouldn't tell you where I'd hidden the phone if I didn't, would I?'

'Hmm.' She considered this. 'I think that might be another reason to like you, John Malarkey,' she said. 'I like being trusted.'

I let her kiss me again − partly for the purposes of the deception, but mostly because I didn't know when I'd get to kiss a girl as beautiful as her again.

I was thinking that she'd tell Cloth exactly what I'd just told her − because the reality was that I refused to trust her − and that it might help take some of the heat off me for a while. I didn't consider for one second that I could be dropping Simon in it.

'Got to go,' I said, and made my escape.

I didn't hang around. But I still didn't know where I was going. I headed upstairs, racking my brains with what I knew about the school's buildings, desperately trying to come up with some kind of hiding place. But I just didn't know the school well enough, and was certain that any hiding place I could think of now, the Tailors would have thought of before me. I was wandering aimlessly, which was dangerous. Where are you, Freddie? I kept asking in my head. Which corner are you waiting round? Where are you going to suddenly jump out from? The school felt as though it was getting smaller and smaller, the net finally closing in. There was no other option left, I had to get out.

I used fire exits to make a rather circuitous route round the school and got as close to the gates on Raymond Avenue as I dared, then kept myself hidden behind a mobile classroom. The bike sheds were deserted but Grunter and Slim were hanging around just outside the gates. Grunter looked as though he was showing the other lad some of his dirty pictures, and Slim seemed excited to see them. It was obvious the other entrances would be guarded too, and I wasn't going to bother risking checking to see, but I had an idea.

With a deep breath and a quick prayer I broke cover and hurried towards the bike sheds on silent feet. I was all eyes and ears, but didn't think I'd been spotted. The Tailors were far too busy to notice me.

The first, second and third bikes were all locked. The fourth had a puncture. The fifth was locked too. I kept checking on Grunter and Slim; they were guffawing loudly. The sixth bike looked as if it had seen better days but there was no lock. I slid it slowly, quietly out of the rack. Grunter was oblivious, but Slim glanced up.

He couldn't have recognized me at first. I saw the frown crinkle his brow but he didn't put two and two together until I was headed for him and pedalling like hell. Then he suddenly started shouting, pointing, but it was way too late. He had to dive for cover as I zoomed past. Grunter didn't even know what was happening until I'd kicked him up the arse and sped by with a whoop.

I didn't stop until I got to the shops on Dean Street. I dumped the bike outside the chippy.

Even here, however, I didn't feel particularly safe. I knew the Tailors came here – Grunter did business here – so kept on the move by wandering the streets around the school. But time was running out for me: the Head of Year was going to have to make a move soon. I wanted to call Cloth again, wanted to push him to send one of his underlings to Mr Coleburn, knowing the longer I left it the more anxious he would get. I just hoped that the more worried Freddie got, the more likely he'd be to agree.

I refused to consider what tenuous logic this actually was.

But I wanted more than that now, didn't I? Revenge for last night; I wanted to hurt them too. Would I be happy with just my innocence any more? Maybe I should call Freddie and threaten him with the phone again, push him further, quicker. Or maybe I should just go through with the threat and see Davie now.

I smoked three cigarettes. I almost wore out the soles of my trainers. Fretting, fretting, fretting. I couldn't stop thinking about Becky. Was she mad, bad, or dangerous to know? Perhaps all three.

I checked my watch again and again. 10.30, 11.00, 11.15. I was losing a lot of time by doing nothing, but told myself to wait it out and let Cloth make the next move. Which was maybe my biggest mistake.

Sixteen

The sudden trilling of the mobile phone startled me. I dug in my pocket for it. 'You found me yet, Freddie?' I asked. But it wasn't the goalie's phone that was ringing, it was mine.

I answered cautiously. 'Hello?'

My mother was crying. The sound of her tears scared me, turned my stomach cold.

'Mum, what's up? Are you okay?'

'Oh, Johnny, they've ripped down the sign. Our beautiful sign.'

'I don't . . . What do you mean, Mum?'

'Some boys have pulled down our sign and smashed it up.'

'But what about the builders? Why didn't they—?'

'They're not here today.' She took a shuddery breath. 'I'm sorry, I . . . It makes me feel so shitty inside, Johnny. Why did they do it? That was Grandma and Grandad's sign too, wasn't it?'

I struggled to answer. I didn't want her to hear my own voice if it betrayed me and broke. 'Mum, I'm sorry. I'm so sorry, Mum.' Because I knew I was to blame.

'It's not your fault, Johnny,' she said, and it almost broke my heart. 'It's me who should be apologizing, calling you at school. You're not in a lesson, are you? I just needed to talk to someone. Tell the teachers it's my fault if they say anything, will you?'

I took a shuddery breath of my own. 'Don't worry.

It's okay. Really . . .'

'It makes me so angry. What a horrible thing to do to us.'

It was making me angry too. It was making me boil. Because I knew exactly which bastards had done it – and why.

'Come straight home from school today, will you?' Mum was asking. 'Let's see if we can fix it, okay?'

'We'll fix it,' I told her.

'It hurts me inside, Johnny. The mindlessness of it.'

'We'll fix it,' I said. 'I promise.'

I managed to stop her from apologizing for calling me, kept telling her it was okay, but it hurt to know how low she must be feeling to have called. She'd never had to call me with anything before. And I'd done this to her. Freddie Cloth had done this to her.

I fumbled with the goalie's mobile until I found the last caller's number. It rang twice before Cloth answered.

'You've messed up this time, Freddie. Real bad.'

'I told you I want that mobile back. Think yourself lucky we didn't put the windows through.'

I was gritting my teeth. 'Do you know why you've messed up? Because I want *you* now, Freddie. It's not just about me clearing my name any more, I'm beyond that. I want *you* personally. I'm going to bring you down.'

'And I should be worried, should I? You're full of it, Malarkey. Bullshit, remember?'

The venom in my voice made me spit froth. 'I'd look closer to home for the bullshit if I was you. Try your girlfriend. Try asking her why she's rubbing herself against me in the lecture theatre.'

His silence spurred me on. I'd stung him. I revelled in it.

'I liked her black bra. Black *and* red; very sexy. Does it turn you on like it did me, Freddie?' I snorted a cruel laugh. 'She's a wild one, eh? I bet you've got to keep a close eye on her, eh?'

His voice was so full of anger he couldn't raise it above a whisper. 'You better be lying to me, Malarkey.'

I laughed at him again. 'I'll steal your girlfriend, then I'll bring your whole gang down. You're not going to know what hit you. You can have my word on it.'

I killed the call with shaking fingers.

TOUCHING CLOTH

SEVENTEEN

'Simon!'

He made to walk right by me. 'Drop dead.'

'*Simon*,' I hissed.

He ignored me.

I was back inside Brook, feeling like I'd flown right back into the spider's web again, and I didn't have time for this. There was only half an hour before the match started.

'Come here!' I snarled as I grabbed his arm, hauling him into the empty classroom.

'What do you think you're—?'

'Shut up and listen.'

'I don't want to have anything—'

I raised a clenched fist. '*Shut. Up.*' But I don't think I would have really hit him. 'And listen.'

He stood with his hands on his hips, as petulant as ever – but quiet at least.

'I need your help,' I told him.

He snorted through his nose at me. 'And why do you think I'd—?'

This time I didn't even need to raise my fist; the look in my eyes was enough. 'I need your help, and in return I'll help you. Okay?'

'The Homework Club?' he asked sheepishly.

'All of it. Freddie Cloth, the Tailors – the whole lot.' I had a loose plan, but wasn't sure how it would all work just yet, wasn't sure if the pieces were going to fit. Not that I was going to admit as much to Simon.

'What are you going to do?' he asked, open-mouthed.

'Destroy it.'

'How?' I liked the awed look in his eyes.

'With your help.'

He nodded. 'Okay.' He hovered awkwardly for a second or two. 'Has it got something to do with your locker?'

That confused me. 'What do you mean?'

'Your locker. Didn't you know? It looks like somebody's broken into it. Was there anything important inside?'

'No, I . . .' But then I remembered Mr Coleburn's paperweight. 'He's got the paperweight.' That was the only thing that tied me squarely to the theft from the Head of Year's office, and I was wondering if Freddie knew it too. If Mr Coleburn found out I had the paperweight I might not be able to clear my name after all; it would be kind of difficult to explain away. And maybe Freddie had blackmail in mind.

Simon, however, didn't seem to know anything. 'Paperweight?'

I ignored the question by asking one of my own. 'Is my locker definitely empty?' Then another thought: 'Has your locker been broken into too?'

Simon shook his head. 'No. Just yours. Why, is somebody going to break into mine?'

'Don't worry about it,' I told him. Maybe I'd judged Becky Chase wrong, I was thinking. But couldn't worry about it too much at the moment. 'Okay, this is what I need you to do—'

'Am I going to get into trouble?'

'Jesus Christ! Will you just shut up and listen a minute?'

I let him go after I'd made sure he knew exactly – *exactly*

– what I needed him to do. Then I wanted to have a look at my locker.

With it being the lunch hour I couldn't exactly sneak around like I had done before. I just had to stay on my guard and keep my eyes peeled. I knew it was risky, but remembered what Cloth had said last night about the risk bringing the excitement – 'the kick' – and was only slightly worried about being able to understand what he meant. I was wary of large groups of kids hanging around in the corridors and made sure I checked trainers before going anywhere near them. I tried to stay hidden in the crowds, avoiding both teachers and Tailors, not wanting to get caught by either. When I reached my locker I saw what I'd been expecting – the door had been forced, the lock broken, the metal bent and twisted. And yes, it was empty.

I was still standing there when I felt a hand grip my shoulder. I thought it was Cloth, and swung round violently, fists ready. But it was worse. It was Mr Macallan.

'Mr Malarkey. Just the person I want to see.' He was already trying to steer me down the corridor, pushing through the groups of kids – towards Mr Coleburn's office, I guessed.

'Mr Macallan, look! Look at that! Someone's broken into my locker. They've stolen all of my stuff!'

'It happens to the best of us,' he growled through his beard. 'Maybe it will teach you a lesson that—'

I played indignant. 'Did you do it, Mr Macallan? Did you do it to get your own back on me?' I was just trying to delay him while I worked out how to get away.

He blew noisily through his thick beard, still shoving

me ahead of him. 'Don't be ridiculous, laddie.' He was jostled by a pair of rowdy, laughing boys. 'Settle down, there! Settle down!' he bellowed.

'Because I didn't steal your wallet, Mr Macallan,' I said. 'Somebody dumped it in my bag.'

'I think I remember this story from yesterday,' he said, glaring at me. 'And I wasn't particularly convinced then, if I remember rightly. I was almost willing to give you the benefit of the doubt. You nearly had me fooled, laddie, I'll give you that. Until Mr Coleburn told me you'd stolen from him as well.' He was lurching me down the noisy corridor, pushing me firmly in the back even as I tried to plant my feet. We were lunch-time entertainment for everybody else. 'I'll insist on the police this time, you can be sure of that. I would have called them already if I was Mr Coleburn. I'd think myself lucky if I were you.'

His pomposity hurt my teeth the way ice cream sometimes does. 'I didn't steal the report cards either.'

But he hadn't been told about those. He pulled me up short. 'What are you talking about?'

I shrugged, playing as dumb as I could get away with. 'The Year Eleven report cards. The ones Mr Coleburn's already signed.' With the furrowing of the maths teacher's brow I suddenly sharpened up. 'Like he probably does every year, because he doesn't give a damn what you teachers write on them. The report cards he's scared parents will find out about.'

The confusion on the maths teacher's face, the bristling of his beard, gave my grey clouds a beautiful silver lining. 'You stole one of Mr Coleburn's paperweights. He's said nothing about any report cards.' But I could see he was thinking about it. I could almost hear the cogs. 'Is this what the so-called "emergency meeting" is all about?'

'You tell me.' We were standing in the middle of the corridor. 'Have you heard of the Tailors, Mr Macallan? They're your bad guys, you know. Have any of you teachers bothered to go near the tuck shop recently?'

'I am tired of your mouth, laddie. I have just about had my fill, and I—'

'You don't know a thing about what goes on in this school, do you?' I asked, honestly amazed, because what Freddie had said last night was all true. The teachers were clueless about what went on here, what the kids got up to behind their backs.

Yet somehow it made a weird sense, because when you considered kids in general, they probably did most of their growing up when adults weren't around. Growing up was a secret, furtive world, out of sight of parents, guardians, teachers . . . I wondered how much my mother really knew about me. I wondered how many lies I'd told her about giving up smoking – and that was just for starters. Then I wondered how many lies Becky had told her father about seeing Freddie Cloth.

I looked around the busy corridor. Most parents would be shocked to discover the kind of shit their kids got away with when their backs were turned.

Mr Macallan hadn't given up trying to march me along just yet. He was huffing and puffing behind his beard. I didn't have a clue whether he was talking to me, himself, or the world in general.

We both looked up to the Tannoy as it buzzed into life. Our favourite Head of Year's voice crackled out: 'Would all Year Eleven tutors please remember to attend the meeting in Mr Coleburn's office. All Year Eleven subject and form tutors. Thank you.'

It only aggravated Mr Macallan even more. He blustered along so hastily he lost his grip on my arm, possibly even forgetting I was there for a split-second as he ranted to himself. I saw my opportunity to get away and took it without a moment's hesitation. I punched the fire alarm.

The corridor was instantly swarming. The tight gangs of kids all burst wide as everybody instantly forgot the fire drill and headed for different exits. A couple of dinner ladies appeared, trying to hustle people in the right direction, shouting orders to beat the deafening bell. It was easy to slip into the middle of it all and leave the maths teacher standing. I knew he'd never be able to pick me out from the throng of uniforms – I was just one among many.

And as I made my way outside with the rest of them, I promised myself this was the last time I'd be running away today. I'd done far too much of it in the last twenty-four hours.

This was going to be the last time I called Cloth as well.

'You've stolen something of mine.'

'Have I?' There was a long pause while I thought I heard muffled voices in the background. He shushed them. 'Didn't think it was worth anything so I chucked it,' he said eventually.

'I want it back.'

'Tit for tat, Malarkey. Funny how you're nicer to me now that I've got something of yours.'

'I'm not joking, Freddie.'

'Can you hear me laughing?'

'I want it back.'

'I want that phone you're using,' he said. 'Maybe we should make an exchange.'

'Okay, at the football match. But I better see what you've stolen from my locker or—'

'Yeah, yeah. Malarkey, Malarkey. Bullshit, bullshit. Just be there yourself.' It was his turn to finish a call for once.

But that was fine by me, as long as he hadn't worked out why I needed the paperweight back.

It might have felt like I was on a runaway train as it hurtled along the track, picking up speed, threatening to come off at the bends, but at least I was taking Freddie Cloth along for the ride. The clever thing was making him believe he was in control.

EIGHTEEN

Brook High were already one–nil down, because Davie still didn't know he was safe. Not that I was taking much notice of the players on the pitch. I didn't feel particularly affiliated to either side and the outcome of the match was the least of my worries.

It was a bright, crisp afternoon; the shouts from the spectators sounding sharp and clear. The whole of Year Eleven were gathered around the pitch, shouting the team on, bellowing at missed opportunities, cheering the best shots. The players blew steam as they charged up and down the field. There was a small group from Stonner who'd come with their team, huddled behind their goalie's net, but Brook made sure their voices were well and truly drowned out. I was standing close to the halfway line, two or three people deep with as good a view around the pitch as I could get. There was a cluster of girls to my left who were complaining about being forced to watch the match, and were trying to encourage each other into disappearing at half-time. Becky Chase was among them.

Not too far away stood a group of teachers, Mr Coleburn included. He was wrapped up in a thick coat and scarf even though it wasn't that cold. He didn't seem to be paying too much attention to the players on the field; he kept looking around, shuffling a few paces forward, a few back. Was he looking for me, or just making sure everybody behaved themselves? I guessed it was probably both. I wondered if he'd handed out fresh report cards to the subject teachers in his emergency meeting. I hoped he was still scared for his own skin.

I hadn't spotted any Tailors yet, and couldn't be sure if they'd seen me or not. I thought I'd probably notice if I was being followed; they'd more than likely want their presence felt because it would be easier to intimidate me. But again, I couldn't be sure. I couldn't take anything for granted. And if there were enough of them in this crowd they'd probably be able to keep tabs on my whereabouts without me knowing a thing about it anyway.

I wanted to stay unnoticed until the last possible moment. That was the plan. I wanted the element of surprise.

Becky had her back to me; I squeezed through the crowd until I was standing at her shoulder. She'd made a promise not to tell Freddie that the mobile was supposedly hidden in Simon Penn's locker, and had kept it, so I reckoned she deserved to be given the chance to be on the side of the good guys when everything went down.

I stood close to her ear. 'Hey, Becky Chase. Enjoying the match?'

She flinched noticeably. The crowd crushed and jostled around us to see a corner being taken at the Stonner end.

'Don't turn round,' I whispered. 'I just need you to point out the guy from Stonner. You know, the one Freddie's supposed to be meeting? Jade's boyfriend.'

I wasn't sure if she'd heard me. I moved closer still. 'Becky?'

She turned her face to me, and I saw the ugly flaring of purple and blue all down the side of her cheek. Her beauty spot was lost within the bruising. And I knew that Cloth had done it. And I knew that he'd done it because of what I'd said. Becky had hidden me from Spike and Big George, she'd kept her promise, and this was how I'd repaid her. It hurt just looking at her.

'God, Becky. I'm . . . Oh God, I'm so sorry.'

She lifted a mobile to her ear, and it wasn't even big enough to cover those horrible bruises.

'No, don't tell him I'm here,' I said quickly, shaking my head. 'Not yet. Please, Becky.'

She lowered the phone slightly. 'Why should I do anything for you?' she asked. Her eyes never left mine. 'Why should I care about anything you say?'

I said, 'It wasn't me who hit you, Becky.' But it felt like a particularly cheap remark, and I was the one who had to lower my eyes first.

'Freddie was right,' Becky said. 'He told me it was *you* who was trying to use me like a puppet.'

'Freddie's not right about anything. Freddie needs somebody to smack him around a bit, to see how *he* likes it.'

She raised the phone again, threatening me. 'Don't you dare!'

'How can you defend him?' I asked, honestly amazed. 'How can you stick up for him now?'

She simply glared at me.

'Come on, Becky, he—'

'He loves me. And I betrayed him because of you.'

'Listen to yourself, Becky. He hit you because I hurt his pride. That's why. He hit you because he's a piece of shit. *That's* why. He hit you because he's too much of a thug to know what else to do.'

She trembled slightly. Maybe because of the wind. 'I'm not listening to you. Why should I? You lie, John Malarkey. You fooled me. I thought you were different. You lie — and you used me.'

I was at a loss to argue back, because, of course, she was right. I couldn't find the words I wanted to say. I was desperate to convince her that returning to Freddie Cloth, going back to him believing she'd deserved a beating, was madness. I stared at her, implored her with my eyes because the words I needed were lost. 'Becky . . .' I tried. 'You . . .' I wanted to say she was too funny and smart and beautiful to fall for this. I wanted to tell her that if he loved her at all, it wasn't in the way she needed. 'Becky, he . . .'

In the end all I could say was: 'Why'd you let the bastard do this to you?'

Her eyes were pale, watery — maybe because of the wind, but I doubted it. And I hated myself for what I'd done to her. I wished I could reverse it.

'You're all the same,' she said. 'You and Freddie and my dad. "String-pullers", that's what I'll call you.'

'Becky . . .'

But she'd finished arguing. She spoke into her phone. 'He's here. Standing right next to me.'

For several long seconds I couldn't move. If I could have made my remorse solid, I would have given it to her, to keep for ever.

She lowered the phone. 'I don't owe you anything,' she told me matter-of-factly. 'I hope Freddie gives you the kicking you deserve. In fact, just kill each other for all I care — and maybe do the whole world a favour.'

Then I was pushing backwards through the crowd,

treading on people's feet, stumbling. 'I'm so sorry, Becky. Really. I'm really sorry.'

I turned to duck and wriggle a way through, but Blondie blocked my path.

The first thing I noticed was his trainers. Still black Adidas, but he'd lost a stripe: all three were white. He'd been demoted and I hoped it was my doing, because of stealing Davie's phone from him. It was such a pity I didn't have the chance to be smug about it.

Dominic Dom and Spike were suddenly there as well. The three of them crowded me, hustled me in the direction they wanted me to go. They forced me right up close to the touchline, where there was nowhere left to run except onto the pitch itself, and they knew I wouldn't want to do that. I glanced around, but I was too far from any of the teachers now for them to see me in the crowd. Becky had turned her back and moved away.

'Give me the phone,' Spike said.

'I want the paperweight first.'

'Freddie's got it.'

I turned to meet his stare. 'Then go get it off him.'

He moved closer, trying to intimidate me, our shoulders rubbing. 'Give me the phone.'

'There's a good boy, Drew. Go fetch the paperweight, eh?'

Blondie barged shoulders with me now. 'You are so dead, Malarkey.'

I didn't even bother to reply. I wouldn't drop my eyes from Spike.

'Watch him,' he told Blondie and Dominic Dom, then moved off through the crowd along the side of the pitch towards Davie's goal. Grunter immediately filled the space he'd left. Where the hell had he popped up from? He didn't look at me, kept his eyes on the game. I made to take a step away, but Slim appeared at my other shoulder. They weren't taking any chances today. They stood firm as the crowd jostled against them. I wanted to know where the others were. Where were Big George and Hutty keeping themselves hidden? There were too many faces in the crowd to see.

I turned to watch Davie. I knew I could do with getting close to him. He didn't look happy; it was obvious his mind was elsewhere. Mr Scapa was bawling at him to concentrate, but he kept fiddling with his gloves, losing track of the ball and looking scared when it came into Brook's half. I had my hand in my pocket, wrapped tight around his mobile.

I looked over at the main block. Before I could do anything I needed a sign from Simon. But there was nothing so far. Had I made a mistake in relying on him?

This was too much of a gamble, I was thinking. Too much could go wrong.

Someone shouted my name above the noise of the crowd. I saw Freddie standing next to the corner flag, watching me. Then the Tailors were moving me again; shepherding me forward. They were forging a way through the crowd, with me at their centre. They didn't care whose toes they trampled, who they pushed aside; they just wanted to get me close to Freddie.

I looked back up at the main block. *Come on, Simon. Where the hell are you?*

I stumbled because I wasn't looking where I was going and nearly fell. Blondie grabbed me before I hit the ground. 'You be careful now,' he told me. 'We don't want any harm coming to you, do we?' He grinned at me maliciously. 'Not unless we do it ourselves.'

Freddie was standing with Becky's friend Jade, and I supposed she'd be taking him to meet her boyfriend as soon as the match was over. 'Show me,' he shouted.

I didn't have much of a choice. I took Davie's mobile out of my pocket and held it up for him to see. Did he still have the paperweight? I wanted to see the paperweight before I did anything else. If he didn't have it then he might have figured out its importance.

But he held it out in front of him, the thick glass catching the sun briefly before he slipped it back into his pocket. He started to move towards me. I didn't want him getting too close.

A quick prayer, then one last glance over my shoulder, and at last I saw Simon's sign. The door to the teachers' stairs – the stairs I'd chased and been chased down when this all started yesterday, the stairs that led up to the roof – was propped open. He'd done his part. So now it was up to me. Now or never. But I had to get away from the Tailors first.

Suddenly the crowd roared; Brook had levelled the score. The crowd of Year Elevens surged like a breaking wave, hands thrown in the air, the noise deafening. As everybody jumped forward, hollered and cheered, I took my chance.

'Davie!' I shouted above everybody else's noise. 'Hey, Davie!' His face was a picture of misery now that his own team had scored – he looked scared. But I was about to put him out of that misery, and when he looked in my direction: '*Catch!*' I threw him his mobile.

Proving he could be a good keeper when he wanted to be, he caught it in his big-gloved hands. He looked at it like it was an alien object, as if it had been dropped straight from a UFO, but seemed to cotton on quick enough. He could save as many balls as he liked now.

Immediately the three Tailors pounced on me. I'd already decided Dominic Dom was probably the weakest link, and brought my elbow back hard into his chin, making him wail, knocking him flat out on his backside. Blondie couldn't get past him as he sprawled, Hutty grabbed my coat, had a grip on me, but I slipped out of the arms and was away, leaving him holding an empty collar. Spike and Freddie were frantically shoving through the crowd towards me. Everybody was still celebrating the goal, jumping up and down and dancing round and hugging each other. I ducked and weaved and twisted away. I wriggled my way through. I was running for the tennis courts. But I wasn't running away, not this time; I was leading Freddie Cloth where I wanted him to go.

Out of the crowd now. I reached the tennis courts and Freddie sounded so close behind me I didn't know if I'd make it or not.

I checked over my shoulder once, when I reached the door to the teachers' stairs. Both Freddie and Spike were after me. Some of the other Tailors were looking bewildered, not sure whether to follow or not, because now the teachers had seen what was going on. I wasn't sure, but I think Mr Coleburn had spotted me. Which was all part of the plan. I charged inside.

Spike and Freddie were getting closer and I led them up the stairs. 'You're dead, Malarkey!' Cloth shouted, his voice booming up the stairwell.

I didn't reply, I saved my breath. I had to get to the top first. If they caught me it would all have been for nothing. I was leaping up two steps at a time, using the banister to haul myself up higher.

I didn't stop at the library, kept on going. My ragged, panting breath bounced off the walls, my heavy footsteps pounded on the stairs.

Freddie and Spike were so close. They were closing in.

At the very top the stairs narrowed; the final flight was boxed in with the walls close on either side. I leaped up the last few steps with what felt like the last squeezed-out drop of energy I had. The red door had a push bar like a fire exit, and I slammed it down, bursting out onto the cold, open roof of the main block.

The wind caught me, tugged at my clothes; it chilled the sweat on my face. I ran across the roof with a view of the whole school below, and beyond the school buildings the surrounding streets and houses. The whole of Brook's world lay before me. It took me a moment's concentration to let a flash of vertigo pass, but in that second my legs threatened to go soft on me. I stamped my feet as if to prove everything was solid and went straight for the box Simon Penn had left for me. It was right on the edge, overlooking the field and the football pitch, exactly as we'd planned.

Freddie and Spike were also on the roof now. Freddie was swearing, spitting with rage. He knew I had nowhere left to run and stopped, bent over, hands on his knees to get his breath back, but he never once took his eyes off me. The fierceness in them was as scary as any vertigo.

'Whatever it is you're playing at, Malarkey, this is it, it's over now. You've got nowhere left to go.' The wind whipped his hair around his face.

I turned to look out over the crowd on the field below. They looked such a long way down, and I didn't like being so close to the edge with Freddie only a few steps away, but I couldn't back out of my plan now. I waved my arms above my head. 'Hey!' I shouted. 'HEY!' I made sure all eyes were on me; I could see Mr Coleburn was already halfway across the tennis courts, heading for the stairs. 'Up here!'

'I don't know what you think you're doing,' Cloth hissed, advancing on me slowly. 'But trust me when I say this is going to end badly.'

I picked up the box. 'Do you recognize this, Freddie?' I asked. I turned it so he could see the words 'MR TAILOR' written on the side. 'It's from the library.'

He turned on Spike. 'I told you to get that,' he spat.

'You said after the match,' Spike replied. 'When we were meeting that kid from Stonner.'

Cloth's eyes were back on me, burning into me. 'Give me the box, Malarkey.' He took a slow, menacing step towards me.

'It's a bit of a struggle to hold,' I said, looking pained. 'What with it being so full of GCSE coursework for Stonner kids, provided by the Homework Club. It's heavy.' I was as close to the edge as I dared get.

'I'm warning you, Malarkey.'

'It's really, really heavy.' I acted up, staggered under the pretend weight. 'I might not be able to hold it much longer.'

'If you don't give me that box, I'm going to—'

I held the box as far out over the edge as I dared

reach. 'Fuck you, Freddie.' Then I tipped it upside down.

The loose bundle of pages fell out in one large chunk. But the wind was quick to pull it apart, pull it away, and scatter the pages. The white sheets twisted and turned as they fell. The wind picked them up and carried them across the tennis courts, the field, the football pitch, the bike sheds. They drifted like massive snowflakes. And the crowd from the football match came running to see what they were. Kids jumped up to grab at the turning, falling whirl of sheets.

Freddie Cloth let out a howl. He could probably see his gang scatter with those pages, see it all falling apart. He was shaking his head in disbelief.

Spike was the same. It took him two or three attempts before he managed: 'Shit, Freddie, we better go.'

But Cloth fixed me with eyes that were on fire. There were A4 sheets blowing across the rooftop, catching around his legs. He ignored everything but me.

I took a step away from the edge. I could tell what was going to happen next.

He roared with rage and hate, screamed at me like a wild animal. He hit me hard and fast, and for one terrifying second I thought we were going over the edge. He was lifting me off my feet. But I managed to twist my body away and he bore me down onto the rough surface of the roof — smashing me down.

He had the paperweight in his fist. I fought him off, rolled away, but he was too quick for me, was on me again. He raised the paperweight high above my head, brought it down hard enough to set off all kinds of fireworks behind my eyes.

194

'Jesus, Freddie! Don't!' It was Spike, scared of what he was seeing.

I held my hands above my head. Freddie brought the paperweight down again. It hammered into my skull. The fireworks died instantly, blackness gobbled them all up. The world spun. The pain was splitting my head in half. I was going, I was losing it. The world was fading.

Then suddenly Mr Coleburn was wrenching on Freddie's arm, dragging him off me. He snatched the paperweight from his hand. 'My God, boy! You could kill him!'

I curled up in a ball. I could see black mist crowding in at the edges of my vision, sucking all the colour away.

Freddie tried to fight on, but was visibly sagging, his eyes going dull. He let himself be pulled away. Pages of coursework blew around his head but he wouldn't look at them.

'What on earth is happening here?' Mr Coleburn wanted to know. He glared at Freddie. He turned to Spike. They wouldn't answer. 'Get this boy an ambulance,' he shouted at Spike.

'I'm okay,' I said, but still wouldn't move. Big Ben sounded in my head if I tried. 'I'll be all right.'

'Do as I say, Buchanan,' the teacher told Spike. 'Then get to my office.'

Spike seemed especially pleased to be allowed to go.

More teachers were appearing on the rooftop. 'I've never seen anything like it,' Mr Coleburn was telling them, his voice shaky, obviously distressed.

'This is GCSE coursework,' said one teacher, who was clutching some of the sheets.

'Who's Mr Tailor?' another asked, looking at the box.

'He was trying to kill that boy,' Mr Coleburn was telling them, his voice suddenly small with shock. 'I've never seen anything like it,' he repeated. 'Never.'

'I'll be all right,' I said. I couldn't sit up just yet, my head was on fire, but the world was returning to me now. 'I'm okay.' I just didn't want to go to hospital, because then my mum would have to be involved. I tried to blink the blackness away. And it worked – kind of.

And that was when Mr Coleburn seemed to realize what it was he was holding. 'Where did you get this?' He took Freddie by the front of his jacket. 'Where did you get this paperweight?' His anger returned in a flood. 'Answer me, boy! Where?'

Freddie looked to me as I rocked slightly with dizziness and pain. 'It's mine,' he said. Glaring at me, still trying to win a victory, thinking I wanted it back. He didn't have a clue. 'It's mine, okay?'

The Head of Year's eyes narrowed. 'Are you sure about that?' He glanced at the teachers around him, as if inviting them to be witnesses to Freddie's words. 'It's *yours*, you say?'

Freddie sneered at me, desperate for even the smallest of triumphs over me. 'Yeah. I said so, didn't I?'

'Then how do you explain the fact that it went missing from my office yesterday?' Mr Coleburn asked. 'And at the same time the report cards were stolen?'

The shock on Freddie's face was so perfect I wished I had a camera. He looked from me to the teacher and back again.

'You stole this from my office, didn't you? Didn't you, boy? When were you in my office?'

Freddie ignored the Head of Year, just kept staring at me. Because he'd suddenly realized now – oh boy, it was so clear to him now.

I winked at him.

My head was pounding louder than a nightclub. I had two huge lumps coming up, each the size of a planet, and making it feel heavy with their weight. Several concerned-looking teachers were crowding around me, frowning, confused, muttering to one another. They gathered in a tight bunch, staring down at me. I lay on my back and gazed up at the sky. Big white sheets of coursework drifted above me. Or were they clouds? I couldn't tell. I needed a cigarette, but couldn't remember where I'd left the packet. Maybe I'd buy some more on the way home. Maybe not. I'd just have to wait and see.

The Fearful

For those who want to believe, no proof is needed.
But for those who can't believe, no evidence is enough.

The legend says that in 1699 schoolteacher William Milmullen and his five pupils visited Lake Mou, but only William returned. He claimed that a terrifying creature rose from the lake and devoured the boys. But did it? And if it all happened so long ago, does it really matter to anyone nowadays anyway?

The legacy of that tragedy lives on in the town of Moutonby. A town divided between those who believe that something terrible still lurks deep down in the lake, and those who don't.

Tim Milmullen wishes he knew. Every day he watches the dark water, looking for a sign. Because if the stories are true, if 'the dragon' in the lake is real, then according to the legend he's the only one who can stop it from killing again.

From prize-winning author Keith Gray comes this powerful, compelling story about why some people believe in things they've never seen, society's intolerance towards others' beliefs, and a father and son trying to understand each other's ways.

978 0 370 32836 2 (from January 2007)
0 370 32836 1

WAREHOUSE

KEITH GRAY

I know a place you can go . . .

'Located in the dockland of a small northern town, the warehouse is a refuge for young people who have slipped through society's safety net. Keith Gray has produced a fast-paced, convincing and moving story.'

ALAN GIBBONS

'Keith Gray's exploration of an invisible sub-culture hits you so hard it almost hurts. It has the power and realism to grip the reader and lead you into a dark, underground world of emotional outcasts.'

DAMIAN KELLEHER

'Grabbing the reader by the scruff of the neck . . . Tough tender and true.'

GUARDIAN

Shortlisted for the Guardian Fiction Award

0099414252

Creepers

Derwent Drive was known as the Speed Creep.
A continual chain of Dashes into the Blind.
If we could make it to the end . . .
we'd be the best.

We'd all heard the story about the Creeper who
dropped Blind into a garden, only to discover he
was standing in a dog pound. It was also the
longest creep around here: twenty-five houses all
in a row, no bends, no kinks. And no Creeper had
ever done the lot. But Jamie and I reckoned we
could do it. Jamie was the best Creeper around.
He was the best buddy you could have.
And he was mine.

**SHORTLISTED FOR THE GUARDIAN
FICTION AWARD**

978 0 099 47564 4 (from January 2007)
0 099 47564 2